THE SLAVE COAST

THE SLAVE COAST

BILL WALL

MERCIER PRESS

First published in 1997 by
Mercier Press
PO Box 5, 5 French Church Street Cork
16 Hume Street Dublin 2
Trade enquiries to CMD Distribution
55A Spruce Avenue Stillorgan Industrial
Park Blackrock County Dublin

© Bill Wall 1997

ISBN 1 85635 196 3

10 9 8 7 6 5 4 3 2 1

A CIP record for this title is available
from the British Library

Cover design by
Penhouse Design Group
Set by Richard Parfrey
Printed in Ireland by ColourBooks
Baldoyle Industrial Estate, Dublin 13

Published in the US and Canada by
the Irish American Book Company,
6309 Monarch Park Place, Niwot,
Colorado, 80503
Tel: (303) 530-1352, (800) 452-7115
Fax: (303) 530-4488, (800) 401-9705

For Peter and Monica Ayles

CONTENTS

In a little time after, amongst the poor chained men, I found some of my own nation, which in a small degree gave ease to my mind. I inquired of these what was to be done with us? They gave me to understand we were to be carried to these white people's country to work for them. I then was a little revived, and thought, if it were no worse than working, my situation was not so desperate. But still I feared I should be put to death, the white people looked and acted, as I thought, in so savage a manner; for I had never seen among any people such instances of brutal cruelty; and this not only shewn towards us blacks, but also to some of the whites themselves.

The Interesting Slave Narrative of the Life of
Olaudah Equiano, or Gustavus Vassa the African
Written by Himself, 1791

1

A NEW WORLD

The *Provident of Boston* backed her topsails and hauled off the quay on the top of the tide on the fifteenth day of March 1799, bound for the New World. When the tugs cast off their lines, she drifted gently past the vast number of boats of every kind that lay at anchor off the busy port called the Cove of Cork. The tide was falling, the first gentle tugging of the ebb, and a light breeze was blowing from the west. An hour before, during the high water stand, one of the harbour pilots had come aboard to steer the ship clear of the mud banks, rocks and shipping. A heavy-set man called Coleman, he had winked at Dónal as though he knew him. He contentedly smoked his pipe as he watched the *Provident*'s preparations with a critical eye, then as the last mooring ropes were taken in hand he took his place by the helmsman and gave the order, 'Let go fore and aft'. The big ropes were let go and hauled aboard and the ship commenced her voyage. As she threaded her way through the shipping he stood by the wheel and called out instructions in a gruff voice, cursing if the helmsman did not immediately respond.

As she cleared the narrow channel formed by the Great Island and the Spit Bank he ordered more canvas, and bigger sails dropped from their yards and were sheeted home. They filled slowly in the breeze and the *Provident* picked up speed, leaning her shoulder into the sea a little. The water began to chuckle against the planks. Then the pilot gave the order to turn down harbour and the sailors were kept busy bracing the yards into the westerly breeze. Now the wooded island of Corkbeg was on the larboard, with its big house and gun battery. On the starboard was Haulbowline Island where the rich men's yachts of the Water Club were spreading their sails. Beyond again were Spike Island and Crosshaven, then the two towering masses of the harbour forts with their huge guns pointed seaward and their lines of red-coated guards.

Dónal Long saw all this. He saw it with the eye of an artist who attempts to record every detail in his memory, for Dónal Long was leaving his native home, and knew that it would be many years before he could see it again. Perhaps, indeed, he would never set foot on Irish soil from this day on. So he stood at the bulwarks and gazed and gazed until his eyes were sore. He stared past Corkbeg at the little cottage on the hillside of Ballymonas where he grew up, where first his mother and then his father had died, where he had lived with his cruel uncle Michael, who was now cook on this very ship, blinded in one eye and half-crippled by the torture he had suffered in the rebellion of '98.

Not too many months before, Dónal himself was in the prison guardhouse in Waterford City, having been arrested under false charges by a brutal yeoman. He had feared for his life and faced torture. Rescued by comrades, he had been brought here to Cove, where a place was found for him aboard this American ship. Captain Pearson of the *Provident* had offered him the job of cabin boy, and so he had found a way to escape the poverty and possible death that awaited him at home.

As the *Provident* passed out between the forts, the harbour entrance was clear. Dónal saw the pilot boat backing her sails about a mile ahead and drifting in their way. As the *Provident* drew nearer, he knew, the pilot boat would free her sails and leap into life, coasting alongside the ship, so close that the pilot could jump into her with complete safety. Now old Coleman relaxed and passed compliments all round, including to the helmsman that he had roundly cursed earlier.

'Where you bound, Captain?' said the pilot as a steaming mug of coffee was handed to him.

'Boston,' was Captain Pearson's reply. 'Madeira first. Then just follow the trade winds I guess.'

'Ah, the trade winds!' The old pilot had a dreamy look in his eye. 'Fine sunny sailing and flying fish on deck.' Dónal was suddenly excited by the notion that he would see these things, that he would make a voyage across the ocean.

'That's it,' the captain smiled.

'But,' said the pilot, 'might you be going to trade along the Ivory Coast? Or the Bight of Benin? I thought you shipped a lot of *brus* and stuff. Trish-trash.'

The captain's face suddenly clouded over. He spun on his heel and stalked to the bulwarks. 'You are too nosy by a mile, pilot. I see your boat is hove to. I reckon you should stand by the ship ladder, we'll be up with her in a moment.'

The pilot chuckled. 'Black gold,' he said. 'It'll rot you, Captain Pearson. There's no luck in that trade! You should have put in at Liverpool or Bristol.'

'Get off my ship, pilot, before I throw you off.'

As the old pilot made his way to the ladder Dónal wondered what the row was all about. The captain had told him they were bound for Boston and he had heard him say so to merchants and visitors alike. Captain Pearson seemed to be a man of his word and so far had treated Dónal fairly. And where was this Ivory Coast and the Bight of Benin? Dónal had never heard of such places but was certain, at any rate, that they were not in Ireland. He did not think they were in England or France either. What was the pilot talking about?

Now the pilot boat was coursing alongside, keeping pace exactly with the *Provident.* Old Coleman climbed over the bulwark and stepped down the ladder, but before his head disappeared over the side he winked at Dónal. 'Watch out for squalls, lad,' he said. 'I know who you are. I knew your father too, God rest him. This ship is not what you think.'

He dropped down the ship's side, stood with one leg on the last step and one hand on the rope, then as lightly as a child he dropped onto the deck of his own boat. The helmsman put the tiller up, the hand eased the sails and the little pilot boat went away to leeward.

Dónal stared after it, racking his brains to know what the pilot could have meant. 'This ship is not what you think.' He went over and over the words he had heard pass between the captain and the pilot so that when he looked up again Roche's Point was astern of them and the coast of Ireland was falling away.

Now the bustle of the ship began to settle down. Sailors went about their business making all safe for sea. Dónal could hear the orders given and repeated, for more sail, for the cargo to be checked again, for the bosun to have the ship's boats double lashed, the anchor to be secured for seagoing, and a hundred other things that were necessary for a ship that was planning a long voyage. So he put his puzzlement behind him and sought out his uncle, who was lying in a hammock, already laid low by seasickness. Captain Pearson had been kind to take Michael Long on as ship's cook and Dónal was grateful to him, but there was no love between Dónal and his uncle; and although they had fished together on Dónal's father's boat in years gone by, Michael Long was no sailor, and the unaccustomed motion of the brig and the brisk seas that were coursing under them had robbed him of what little sea-legs he possessed. He was too weak to talk and Dónal stood by him for half an hour or so, telling him all the time that the first three days at sea were the worst and that he would soon recover, that very soon they would be in America and he would never again have to set foot in a ship. Every now and then his uncle was sick into a wooden bucket that someone had hung from the same beam as the hammock and eventually Dónal was unable to stick the smell and the sound any longer and went back on deck.

He was hailed by Mr Burgess, the first mate. 'Long, the cap'n wants you. Move along there.' Mr Burgess was a gruff man and rarely gave an order without making it sound like a threat. Dónal moved quickly out of his way as he stalked forward.

The captain was sitting in his cabin with the logbook in his hand. He smiled broadly when Dónal entered.

'Well, mister, I'm mighty pleased to see you. This will be a lucky voyage, I'm sure of it. Where do you think we're bound?' Dónal was about to say that he had the captain's word that they were bound for Boston when the captain cut him short. 'Why Boston, for sure. Boston.' He hooted with laughter. 'Boston is a capital place for a young fellow like you. And I'll have you set up like every man in this crew. For sure I will.' He clapped his hands and rubbed them together. 'Coffee, mister. I require coffee this instant.'

Dónal's main task as cabin boy on the *Provident* was to serve at the captain's table, as he had been instructed when he signed on in Cove. But he had never made coffee in his life. He looked blank.

'Do you want a start, mister?'

Dónal stammered out that he had never tasted coffee, much less brewed it, and the captain laughed loudly again. 'Tea, by God, I'd say you Irish drink tea.' He leaned forward and stared Dónal in the eye. 'Sheer poison to a Yankee. We never drink anything but coffee. Not since '73. We threw all the tea in Boston Harbour. I'll show you once but I won't show you twice.'

Dónal thanked him. 'I would like to do my duty, sir. But I know I must learn and I'm right ready to do that.'

'That's the spirit,' the captain said. 'A man after my heart.'

Dónal learned to grind the coffee beans the way the

captain wanted it done, and to brew the black foul-tasting liquid, but he could never understand why anyone wanted to drink it. He also learned how to set out a table with knives and forks and to clean them properly, how to polish brass and wash clothes, how to wait on table, and a hundred other lesser things. As days advanced at sea he settled into his new found tasks without too much difficulty, and he was relieved to see that his uncle had recovered from his seasickness and was regarded by the men as a competent cook.

The days did not hang heavy for Dónal. Firstly he was at sea where he had always longed to be, even if he was only a cabin boy. Then he was bound for America where he had high hopes of making his fortune. Furthermore Captain Pearson kept his word, given at the Cove of Cork, and gave him daily lessons in Latin, mathematics and navigation, and Dónal could not have asked for a more patient teacher.

'You have brains and education, mister, and God forgive you if you waste them. I'm going to teach you the way I taught my own boy!'

The captain often told him about his son, who went to sea just like Dónal. He had risen to the rank of mate and was indeed a fine seaman and navigator. But the ship he sailed on had foundered in a gale off Cape Hatteras and only three men survived, drifting for weeks in a lifeboat before they were picked up. His son was not one of them.

'The sailors' rhyme is well spoken, Dónal. "If Tortugas let you pass, beware, beware Cape Hatteras." It was Cape Hatteras that got my boy William.'

For three hours every morning they struggled together with Latin verbs, with geometry and with the basics of chart-work and observations. Dónal was instructed in the delights of using a sextant, the complicated instrument which measured the angle between the horizon and the sun or moon, and which was used to fix a position, and marvelled that while the captain's readings showed them to be progressing steadily southwards in the Atlantic, his own numbers placed them at various ridiculous points on the globe, from Tahiti to central Russia. When he complained that he would never learn to use the sextant, Captain Pearson simply told him that practice was all. 'Keep at it, mister. I ain't so long in the tooth that I can't remember when I made the same mistakes. You'll learn. Keep at it.'

Once when they were poring over a huge chart, happily inserting the captain's latest noonday position, Dónal asked about their course. So far the *Provident* had sailed steadily southwards towards the equator. They had not made a single mile westwards towards the New World.

The captain smiled and said that they were sailing south to catch the trade winds that would blow them towards America. 'South to the sun, mister. For sure as far as Madeira. Maybe even the Cape Verdes. Madeira is a beautiful place. Then the happy days running down the trades. Flying fish on the deck. Never a hand to the sails for days on end, just the steady blessed trade winds at our back. I remember it when I was a boy, on my father's ship. The sun and cooling breeze. So it's south, Mr Long. South for the trades.'

'As far south as the Bight of Benin?' Dónal asked. He

still remembered the pilot's remarks.

The captain looked at him sharply. 'You know nothing of the Bight of Benin, mister. Stick to your navigation.' He stared at Dónal for a moment then slammed the ruler and dividers he had been using onto the floor and turned his back completely. 'The only Bight you'll hear about, mister, is the bight of a rope.'

The captain did not recover his cheerful mood. In a few minutes he dismissed Dónal, a good half hour before the lesson usually finished.

Dónal got to know his shipmates quite slowly. This was a consequence of his position as a cabin boy and the fact that he slept in a room that was little more than a cupboard right next to the captain's cabin. The sailors, on the other hand, slept forward in the forecastle where they kept a constant fire going in a battered old stove while Dónal shivered under meagre blankets in his draughty box. Mr Burgess, of course, he got to know from serving him at the captain's table. And he made the acquaintance of the second mate, Mr Munro, who was an altogether soft-hearted man by comparison with Burgess. Everyone said that Burgess was a 'driver', meaning he pushed the men hard all the time, but that Munro was a 'decent skin' even if he was 'a little too much in the religious line' for them. Nevertheless, it seemed to Dónal that none of the three officers was as bad as Mr Wilson of the *Leander*. Mr Wilson was the man who had plotted against his life and who had killed his best friend. He was the first officer of the Royal Navy man-of-war on which Dónal had served as powder monkey. He was so bad that several of the sailors had vowed to kill him and even the captain didn't like him.

Captain Pearson, Burgess and Munro all seemed to Dónal to be decent officers and respected, if not liked, by the men. That was all he wanted, because this ship was merely to be the means by which he would fulfil his dream of reaching the New World.

Two strange things happened on their passage south.

The first was an argument in the dead of night between Mr Burgess and the captain.

Dónal had been asleep in his cabin and as usual had slept through the watch bells, which were rung every half hour, but which Captain Pearson muffled up at night. So when he woke he had no clear notion of the time and at first he couldn't understand why he was awake at all. It seemed to him that he had heard strange noises, voices raised in anger and the sound of furniture falling. He listened to the ship's sounds, the singing of the waves against the planking, the creak of blocks and rigging, the groaning of the steering gear. All seemed normal. He was convinced he had dreamed it all and was turning over in his cot when he heard the voices again. Now he was wide awake.

The voices were coming from the captain's cabin. They were no longer shouting, but Dónal knew they were the same voices that woke him from his sleep. There was only a thin partition between his cabin and the captain's and he put his ear to it to listen. The voices were muffled and he could make nothing out, though he could hear the bitterness between them. Out of curiosity he crept out and took up station just outside the door to the captain's cabin. Now he could hear snatches of what was being said.

Burgess sounded drunk and his words were indistinct, but Dónal heard him tell the captain that he was a liar. He was astonished to note that the captain, instead of hitting him, was speaking softly to him, wheedling him.

'Davey, Davey, it had to be done. Would you have shipped with me again if I did not? This is the last one, Davey. We'll all be made out of this one. I ain't fooling this time. Why, I have a tidy profit already.'

'Damn profit!'

'That's not so easy to say, Davey. I have a wife and family. And so have you.'

Mr Burgess spoke but Dónal could not make out his words.

'No such thing,' said the captain in a louder voice. 'The Bible approves it. It is no sin, by God. Looky here, Davey, we have Cape St Vincent on the larboard right now. Would you have me turn tail and sail for Boston with a cargo of trash?'

Suddenly the mate's words were clear and loud. 'I will not go to hell for you or any master! Damn you, Nathaniel Pearson! I'll see you swing yet.'

The captain, equally loud: 'And I'll have you in irons as quick as you can say jack snipe!'

Dónal heard the sound of a chair scraped back suddenly.

'Put down your knife, you fool!' This was Captain Pearson, anger gone from his voice, replaced by something very like fear. 'You'll hang for mutiny, no matter what my crime is!'

A loud thud followed and the door was flung open. Mr

Burgess staggered out, brushing Dónal aside, and as the door swung slowly back with the roll of the ship Dónal caught a glimpse of the interior.

Captain Pearson was standing at his table. A huge knife such as Dónal had never seen before, almost a sword, was stuck deeply into the wood and still quivering slightly from the force of the throw. Captain Pearson was staring at the door, almost exactly into Dónal's eyes, but Dónal knew from the strange look in them that he did not see him. He was staring at the space where he had last seen Burgess.

The second strange event concerned a school of dolphins.

One beautiful day, with the wind broad on the beam and the sun whitening everything, a school of dolphins came to play alongside the boat, and Dónal, who was on deck at the time, rushed to the side to watch them. They kept pace with the ship and seemed to enjoy plunging in the bow-wave and criss-crossing in front of her. He had no particular work at that moment and so he swung his legs over the bow and stood on the bowsprit where he could best watch their antics. There were about twenty of them and they were amazingly playful. So much so that Dónal was convinced they were aware of his presence and were showing off to him. Time passed as he watched them and he lost track of the happenings on the ship until he saw the captain coming forward off his quarterdeck with one of the younger sailors who was carrying a huge musket, a bag of shot and a cow's horn of powder.

Dónal sprang back onto the deck. 'Oh Captain,' he cried. 'You do not mean to shoot them!'

Captain Pearson grinned. 'They make fine eating, Dónal. That lubber of an uncle of yours can cook dolphin, I suppose. If not, I'll have him over the side. Stand here, Gideon Blood,' he told the young sailor. 'No easy shots now. I want to see your famous marksmanship. See that one away out there? Could you take me that one?'

The young man nodded and threw the gun to his shoulder. He sighted carefully along the barrel then cocked the firing hammer with his huge right hand. It seemed to Dónal that the gun was at least a foot longer than the sailor himself and as heavy as lead. He watched in horror as the man's finger tightened slowly on the trigger. There was a tremendous bang and the sailor was jerked backwards, almost causing him to stumble. Dónal's eyes swung out to the distant dolphin and he saw blood in the water. At the same time he heard the captain shouting for Burgess.

'Heave to, Burgess! Back your headsails!'

There was a mad rush of footsteps to carry out the order, Burgess shouting, 'Helm a-lee!' and the helmsman spinning the wheel and shouting back, 'Helm's a-lee!' The brig was rounding slowly up to wind and losing speed.

'Boat!' shouted the captain. More rushing feet. The young sailor was rapidly reloading his musket. Looking at the dolphin again, Dónal could see him slowly making his way along the surface, leaving an ugly red stain on the water. 'Fire again, Gideon Blood. Fire again, damn you!' Another loud bang and a spurt of water and blood on the dolphin's back. The davits had been swung out and a boat was lowering over the side.

The captain was gleeful. 'Two hits, Gideon Blood. That

gun of yours is nearly a cannon!' The boat was pulling away towards the bloody patch of sea. 'A fine shot, Blood. A good shot. A Kentucky shot, I'd say, wouldn't you, Mr Burgess?'

Mr Burgess shrugged his shoulders. 'I reckon it was, Cap'n.'

'Come now, Mr Burgess. Ain't this Gideon Blood a crack shot? Sing out, man. Ain't he?'

'A crack shot, Cap'n. It was a crack shot.' Burgess spun on his heel and began shouting at the men bracing the yards.

The captain clapped Gideon Blood on the back and told him he would have dolphin steaks for his supper, a prospect that did not seem to please Gideon Blood. 'I'd appreciate it if I could put my gun away, Cap'n,' was his only reply. At a nod from the captain he carried the huge musket back to the fo'c'sle ladder and disappeared below.

'God damned Kentuckian!' the captain cursed. 'But what a shot!'

That night they had dolphin steaks in the captain's cabin and it was all Dónal could do to stop himself crying at the sight of them. But before he had to eat some himself he heard the lookout shout, 'Sail ho!' and Mr Munro's answer of 'Where away?' In an instant the captain and Mr Burgess had flung their coats on and were rushing into the night air.

2

THE TRIANGLE TRADE

Captain Pearson and Mr Burgess consulted with Mr Munro, the officer of the watch. The ship was deathly silent, most of the hands standing quietly in the waist of the ship and staring up to windward. Dónal looked up, and there in the moonlight less than half a mile away were the ghostly white sails of a British warship, gliding down on them in the gentle breeze.

'How did she come up with us, Mr Munro, unseen?'

'It looks bad now, sir, moonlight and all, but ten minutes back there was no moon. Those clouds made it black as hell.' He gestured towards the massive bank of cloud that was drifting away eastwards. 'When we saw her first it was only the bow-wave that gave her away.'

'Has she seen us?'

'Yes, sir. She altered course to bring us under her lee. She means to speak us.'

Mr Burgess was studying her through a spyglass. 'Will we run, Cap'n?'

'Too late, Mr Burgess. And besides we would only

advertise ourselves as troublemakers.'

'We could outrun her.'

'I'd say we're in range of her great guns and I ain't about to risk it. Let them board. We'll give them coffee.' All three grinned.

'She's a frigate,' Burgess said, almost to himself.

An hour later, all the appropriate signals having passed between the ships, the *Provident* was hove too within hailing distance of the warship. Dónal could see the battle lanterns burning between the decks where the gun crews were standing by, ready to run out their guns and fire on them. He remembered the happy days he had spent aboard the *Leander*, the comradeship of the sailors, the efficiency of the gun crews, their courage and loyalty. He wished he could simply leap into the sea and swim to her, begging her captain to take him aboard so that he might be a powder monkey again. That was what his heart wanted, but then his brain would tell him that his best chance lay with Captain Pearson and America. So he simply stood on the quarterdeck and watched as the captain crossed in one of the ship's boats and stepped aboard the British vessel.

Everyone else was watching too, if they did not have work to do. His uncle had come on deck, wiping his hands on a filthy apron. His one eye was staring intently at the British ship. There was something about his uncle's behaviour that Dónal could not quite place. Perhaps he was worried that the British officers were coming to arrest him. Or was there something else, something Michael Long knew that Dónal didn't? In fact, now that he noticed it, everyone was nervous. Sailors who should have been below decks asleep in their hammocks had found excuse to be where they could keep an eye on the warship, fiddling with ropes, adjusting the knots on the water-breakers, shifting belaying pins. Not so long ago America was at war with England, Dónal thought, and these men are still uneasy about it.

He saw a boat set out from the British ship with a party of sailors and marines and a lieutenant in the stern sheets. He saw them come aboard and heard them declare to Burgess and Munro that they intended to search the ship. Ever since the American War of Independence there was a strong dislike between American and British ships, and British men-of-war used almost any excuse to stop and search vessels flying the stars and stripes.

But no one raised any objection to the search. Dónal heard Munro offer coffee to the lieutenant and the offer was accepted.

Munro called to Dónal to fetch the captain's pot and three cups, and when he arrived back on deck with it the two mates and the naval officer were standing on the quarterdeck chatting about the weather. Below decks, he knew, the marines were searching the hold, and shortly they would report. In the meantime the three men chatted quietly.

Dónal thought there was an air of unreality about the scene. Here were two ships a thousand miles from port, rising and falling on a gentle swell, their masts and sails silvered by moonlight, their officers politely drinking coffee and discussing the possibility of there being more wind tomorrow.

Then a marine sergeant snapped to attention in front

of the lieutenant and said: 'Nothing to report, sir. Hold clean. Cargo of guns, cloth, odds and ends of brass and so forth. The usual, sir.'

'Very good, sergeant. Carry on.' Dónal remembered the casual way that orders were given aboard the English ships. It was as if every man knew his part before ever he was told.

The marine clumped down to the waist and marshalled his men over the side and into their boat. Then the lieutenant thanked the two mates and climbed over the side in his turn. As they rowed away across the silvery sea Burgess and Munro grinned broadly at each other.

It was not long before Captain Pearson's boat was seen pulling away from the warship again, the wet oar blades gleaming in the moonlight. She had hardly pulled twenty yards before the warship was under way, yards braced and headsails taut. Like a huge shining whale she eased through the sea and drew ahead of the *Provident*, the lights of her battle lanterns disappearing as the gunports closed. Dónal could easily imagine the men securing their guns and turning in wearily for a few more hours' sleep.

When Captain Pearson came aboard, Munro laughingly told him that they had indeed given the British officer coffee. 'And he never guessed a thing.'

Even Burgess was laughing. 'The fool stood here talking about the weather. All cotton between the ears!'

The captain scowled at them. 'It was not as easy as that! Why do you think I took so long to get back? That fool of a British officer with cotton between his ears reported that he wasn't quite happy with the ship. "I can't quite say," says he, "but she is carrying a cargo of guns and bric-a-brac." Guns and bric-a-brac!'

Burgess and Munro were silent.

'I told him I was bound for the Guinea coast with guns for the King of Dahomey. "What are these guns to be paid for in?" says he. As if I was going to say slaves! "Gold," says I. "The King of Dahomey is a very rich man."'

'They believed you?'

'They did not, but what could they do about it. Make sail Mr Munro. Let us be off.' He stalked off to watch the British ship as she crowded on sail, heading east. 'Mr Munro, their captain told me that he was dead set against the slave trade, a follower of Wilberforce, if you please. He declared that he did not think I was a merchant brig at all but what he called "one of those damnable slavers"! Imagine that! Imagine the British thinking my *Provident of Boston* was a slaver!' Dónal heard that hooting laugh again and saw Munro and Burgess exchange knowing glances.

'Mr Long, I'll take a plate of ship's biscuit and a glass of water on deck here. That weevilly biscuit your uncle serves up.'

The days stretched out again. The tropical seas were mainly calm, the skies clear, the sailing easy. Dónal went about his work with a will, serving at table, lending a hand on deck when he was needed. In the evenings he met his uncle by the mainmast shrouds where they would stand and talk, wondering together at the warmth and comparing it with home, discussing the crew and the officers and the happenings of the days.

Gideon Blood he knew well from the shooting of the dolphin, but that incident had so revolted Dónal that he found he could hardly speak to the young man. Blood's best friend was Joe Quane, and they both hailed from the state of Kentucky. Quane was as short and fat as Gideon Blood was long and thin. They made a strange pair talking by the anchor bitts, but in time Dónal grew accustomed to them and often found himself included in their conversations. Quane had been a riverboat sailor on the Ohio river at one time, but Gideon Blood was the son of a farmer and had never set foot on a boat until he shipped aboard the *Provident*. Quane talked all the time, mainly about life on the Ohio and the people he had known there. Blood didn't say much, preferring to concentrate on the thick lump of chewing tobacco he always had in his mouth.

Dónal was curious about why he, a farmer's son, had gone to sea, and once he asked him straight out.

Gideon Blood stopped chewing, manoeuvred the lump of tobacco into the corner of his mouth and looked into Dónal's eyes. 'Run away.'

Dónal had run away too. 'Why did you run away, Gideon Blood?'

'Killed a man.' The tobacco came back between his jaws and he started to chew again. Dónal was so taken aback that he could hardly think what to say, but Quane laughed.

'That big old gun. Why it'd blow a hole in a house. I guess you made a mighty hole in him, Gideon Blood?'

They both looked at Dónal, who watched fascinated as the tobacco was shifted again.

'Blowed his whole head off,' Gideon Blood said. 'Like that.' Suddenly he made an explosive sound and spat the tobacco lump straight into Dónal's face. Shocked, Dónal fell backwards off the coil of rope he was sitting on and rolled on the deck, desperately wiping his face. Then they roared laughing, pointing at him like children.

Eli Twiss was the ship's carpenter. Sometimes he would let Dónal sit in his little carpenter's shop right forward in the bows. The room was little more than the length and breadth of a coffin, and the wood being dark with Eli's pipe smoke, it resembled a coffin in more ways than one. Eli had been at sea as long as he could remember.

'Man and boy, more'n fifty year, I reckon. Reckon old Nick'll have to come for me hisself when he wants me and I hope he kin swem!'

Dónal enjoyed the carpenter's stories but often found it difficult to understand his accent. Eli had a fund of tales about everything to do with the sea and he enjoyed having a boy to listen to them. Dónal heard him tell of the cannibal isles of the pacific and the Caribs of the South American Coast who broke the legs of their prisoners so that they could eat them later at their leisure. He had seen the island of Bouvet in the South Atlantic which appeared and disappeared from time to time, a fact which no philosopher could explain, according to the carpenter. He had seen the islanders of Fiji cooking a white man, which they called 'long pig' because the white man's skin was the same colour as a pig's. He had seen an octopus with arms one hundred feet long and a whale whose head was as tall as the ship.

Dónal listened in awe to these tales, thinking that here at last was a real sailor. And in truth, Eli Twiss had been around the world more than once. He had passed Cape

Horn in fair weather and foul more often than he could remember. He had sailed aboard his first ship when he was but a lad of eight years and now he was so long at sea that he 'couldn't sleep one night in a feather bed.'

This however was his first trip with Captain Pearson. 'Cain't say I likes it, Dónal. I signed on for the voyage to Ireland and back. Cargo o' New England rum in, Irish butter out. But, looky you, no butter.' This last part was delivered as if it were final proof of something terrible.

'I don't see what's wrong with that, Eli. Maybe the price of butter was too high?'

Eli Twiss chuckled grimly. 'Ever heerd o' the triangle trade, boy?' Dónal shook his head. 'Weel, this here is how it happens. Out of Liverpool or Bristol or your old Cove of Cork, a cargo o' guns an' cotton an' bracelets or suchlike to Africa. Then a cargo o' black slaves to Jamaica. Cargo o' molasses or sugar cane to Boston to make the rum an' start all over again.' Dónal did not like to point out that since the *Provident* had already sailed from Boston to Ireland there were four lines in the trade and that therefore it was not a triangle.

'But are you saying this is a slaving voyage, Eli Twiss? For shame. I heard the captain himself say it was not when the English officer was aboard that night. I heard him say so to the mate.'

Eli Twiss tapped his forehead with his index finger. 'You'll b'lieve it when yah sees the barracoons, boy,' and he turned away to work on the coopering of one of their huge water barrels.

Mr Munro, the second mate, was forever quoting the Bible. Every Sunday morning he conducted a prayer service in the fo'c'sle which all the men resented because it went on so long and because Mr Munro preached a very long sermon. For the remainder of the week he was a decent officer, very rarely using violence to make the men work harder. He was unlike Mr Burgess in that way. Burgess carried that wicked long knife that Dónal had seen and besides he had a length of thick rope with which he thumped anyone who was moving too slowly for his liking. He 'started' Dónal, as he called this practice, once or twice and Dónal quickly learned to jump to his work and keep out of the mate's way.

The men usually sang as they worked, the rhythm of the songs helping to keep them working together. There was one song, though, that they sang with great delight and with much nodding and winking to each other:

> O was you ever in the Congo River,
> Shallow, shallow brown.
> Where fever makes the white man shiver,
> Shallow, shallow brown.

Sometimes the song simply told of the men's pride in being the crew of 'a Yankee clipper', but other times, especially when the work was hard and the singers added extra verses, Dónal heard words that he only half understood. When he asked Eli Twiss about them, the old carpenter shook his head and said Dónal would see soon enough.

A spell of bad weather put all thought of navigation lessons out of Dónal's mind. They struggled with the ship and the sea and neither the stars nor the sun or moon did they see while the gales battered them. Captain Pearson worked his ship with great skill and Dónal could see that Munro and Burgess were fine officers, each able to do his part. The men too were all prime seamen. It was a well-found ship and Dónal was pleased that he had found his way onto this fine vessel, where he made no doubt he would learn his trade to perfection.

The moonlit night on which they met the British ship came at the end of the last tranquil day's sailing for more than a week, so that when the fine days resumed Dónal was amazed to see that they had passed the Cape Verde Islands and were beginning to turn gently eastwards. He was worried by this, but remembering the way that the captain had been angered by his previous question about their destination, he made up his mind to pick his time and do some navigation of his own without the captain's knowledge.

It was becoming intolerably hot, though the rest of the crew did not seem to mind, and he had taken to sleeping on deck in the shelter of the bulwarks. This was how he was awakened by the slapping sound of something landing on the deck quite close to him. When he opened his eyes he found himself looking directly at the face of a fish. He was startled and sat up so quickly that he thumped his head. Almost at the same moment three more fish landed on deck within twenty feet of him. Sore as well as startled now, he contemplated what he thought was a kind of mackerel with wings until he realised it must be his first flying fish. 'You look a bit like Mr Munro,' he mused. He turned it over in his hand and marvelled at the outstretched triangular fins with which the marvellous creature glided high enough to fly over the bulwarks of the *Provident of Boston*. The fish continued to land at irregular intervals with a disturbing slapping sound along the deck, and Dónal knew he would not sleep there that night. He decided to return to the cot in his cabin where he could expect some peace even though the air below would be stifling.

The captain's snoring could be heard as far as the main companionway. Dónal thought of the charts they had been working on a few hours before, carefully rolled in their leather holders and stowed along the shelves in the captain's cabin. Now is my chance, Dónal thought. He opened the door gently and saw Captain Pearson thrown back on his bunk, his head tilted back, his mouth open, one arm flung out over the side of the bed, the other jammed behind his head. For a moment Dónal almost laughed aloud at such a comical way of lying down. There was a strange sweet perfume in the air and he wondered that in the time he had been serving in this cabin he had not noticed it before. Then he made his way silently to the chart table and reached for the latest charts.

He placed them on the table and, using the ruler, laid out a line from their present position following their present course. It ran off the chart so he pulled out the next one and continued the line, finding that it finished up on the coast of Africa. There was little enough light at the table so he took the chart to the stern window where a reflection of the moonlight showed him that his line finished at a slight inward curve of the coast. He was just able to read the words 'Bight of Benin'.

So old Coleman, the pilot in Cork Harbour, was right

after all. The ship was bound for Benin, the Slave Coast, and with a cargo of guns. But what for? And was this just another stop in the voyage to America? Perhaps the captain meant to keep his bargain after all. Or perhaps, as Eli Twiss had said, this really was a slave ship.

Suddenly he became aware that the captain's snoring had ceased. He felt the hairs on the back of his neck prickle. Slowly he turned round, hoping to slip back to the chart table and out through the door. He saw the captain sitting up on the edge of his bed, his eyes burning as bright as lamps and directed straight at Dónal's. One hand was clutched tightly to his nightshirt at his neck.

'Captain, I . . . ' he began.

'A trifle cold tonight,' the captain interrupted him. His voice was pleasant, familiar, yet it frightened Dónal for some reason.

Dónal did not think it was cold. Sweat was coursing down his face now, and the tropical air was so hot he felt his lungs would not fill. He stood where he was, in the light of the stern windows, paralysed by fear.

'No matter,' the captain continued, quite calmly. 'We will treat them well in the Middle Passage. And remember they will be Christians at the end of it. Yes, souls saved from paganism. Not too many, so the yellow jack and the smallpox doesn't ruin us. I calculate twenty per cent at the worst.'

Dónal was confused. What was the captain talking about? What twenty per cent?

'I was just consulting the charts,' he said, hoping that the lie would be enough to save him from the captain's wrath. 'Practising my navigation. I couldn't sleep.'

'For sure, you know where we are now. Goodnight. I am very tired this time. Very tired.'

The captain did not lie down. Dónal saw the eyes, still as bright as before, move slowly over the room and come to rest on the compass that was balanced above the chart table – the 'telltale compass' the men called it. 'Southwest by west,' he said.

Dónal placed the charts carefully on their shelves, noticing as he did so that their course was not southwest by west, and turned again to face the captain. 'Good night, sir,' he said, but now the captain's eyes were closed though he was still sitting on the edge of his bed.

Dónal tiptoed out of the cabin and shut himself into his own room with relief. He did not sleep that night but lay awake terrified by the knowledge he had obtained – that the unlucky ship in which he had his made his escape from Ireland was that most horrible of things – a slave trader. Nothing could reconcile his mind to that thought and he agonised for hours thinking that had he taken heed of what was being said earlier he might have volunteered to serve on the British man-of-war as was his right. He was equally terrified by the thought of what the captain would do when the cold dawn light brought back the image of Dónal standing in his cabin. He listened all night, hoping to hear the snores again because the snoring would tell him that he was safe from the captain's wrath for the time being at least. But the eerie silence continued and Dónal lay awake until the watch bell told him that daylight was at hand.

3
—

MERCHANDISE

Their days continued as before and the captain seemed to have no memory of seeing Dónal with the charts. Instead he continued his lessons and Dónal watched the course line draw inexorably closer to the Bight of Benin. As time went on Dónal became more expert at the sextant work and by now could usually fix their position within fifty miles. This, the captain assured him, was not bad at all.

As they neared the African coast Dónal was surprised to see that there was no natural harbour ahead of them. Instead there was a low-lying shore with sandy beaches as far as the eye could see. The Atlantic breakers fell on this shore in an explosive surf line, threatening with complete destruction any ship that got too close. How could they land here? Their cargo would have to be taken off in boats and even those boats might be smashed to pieces in the waves.

They dropped anchor about a mile off shore, well outside the surf, and the captain ordered one of the ship's boats lowered. By now an air of gloom had settled on the ship. Every face was closed to Dónal and he could not raise a smile or a word from any of them. They went about their tasks in silence.

Dónal was to go in the boat, and Gideon Blood, and four others besides the captain. They were each provided with a sword and pistol, and Gideon Blood had his huge musket. They cast off and pulled for the shore, and as they approached the boiling white line Dónal began to see that the four sailors who pulled on the oars had done this before. They managed the boat expertly along the breaking waves, following the crests as far as possible, in such a way that almost no water came over the side.

Then they were out in the surf and running in with the boat gripped firmly so that as the last wave dragged back out to sea they heaved her onto the wet sand. Dónal saw the next great breaker rushing towards him as Gideon Blood grabbed his arm and pulled him bodily into the water.

Before the wave broke, the boat was hauled up onto the dry sand. Dónal and Gideon Blood set about hauling her further and securing her by a rope around the stump of a tree. It took them some time, and when he turned round to look for orders Dónal found that the captain and the four oarsmen had disappeared.

'Hi, Gideon Blood, where's the captain! We're marooned!'

Gideon Blood spat into the sand and said that their job was to wait here and watch the boat.

'But where are they gone, Gideon?'

'To the barracoons to meet the trader.' Gideon looked at him as if he should have known it.

'What are these barracoons?'

'Where the "flesh", as they calls it, is kept. The black-birds. Negroes.'

Gideon Blood turned his back on Dónal, cradled his gun in his arm and settled down to watch the thin scrub that bordered the beach. Clearly Dónal could not expect any further information. He wondered that even Gideon Blood could call other human beings 'flesh' and 'black-birds', though he had heard these words used frequently by the sailors in recent days.

They waited all afternoon and Gideon Blood did not utter a word in that time, except to warn Dónal not to stray from his sight. That was when Dónal, tired of the waiting and exhausted by the heat, had decided to sit in the shade of a tree a little further back.

He must have fallen asleep there in the cool of the shade because he was awakened by the arrival of one of the oarsmen, trampling through the brush like a horse, red in the face and out of breath from running.

'Make the signal, Gideon Blood,' he shouted from a long way off. 'Make the signal. They have the flesh!'

Gideon Blood cocked his musket and pointed it straight into the air and Dónal heard again that crash and saw the smoke and flame spout from the barrel. Then all three of them stared at the *Provident*. The signal was answered shortly by a puff of smoke and the sound of a gun on the ship. Then Dónal saw the boats being lowered over the side and noticed that most of their cargo had been stowed on deck ready to be put ashore. Now tackles were used to swing the cargo out and lower it into the boats. As soon as the boats were loaded they cast off and the flash of the oars told Dónal that their crews were rowing fast towards the shore.

Three hours later darkness had fallen like a curtain over everything, and the darkness had filled up with sound, shrieking and chattering and roaring. Dónal was terrified.

The sailors had brought the cargo ashore safely, except for one boat which had overset in the surf and which had been smashed to pieces. Most of its cargo of cotton had been recovered, though, and none of the sailors had been lost. They had stacked the cargo on the beach to wait for the captain and the slave trader to come for it. Then they had all piled back into their boats and rowed for the ship as fast as their oars could move them, leaving Dónal and Gideon alone as before. Just before dark Gideon had made a pile of driftwood, some of it from the smashed boat, some way away from the cargo, and using the paper-dry grass and some gunpowder, he had made a fire. He advised Dónal to 'set near the fire' and he would not be troubled by animals for the night and so Dónal had fallen asleep again in the heat and light, thinking of happier days at home. His last memory before drifting off was of the warm fire in the hearth in the cottage where he grew up, and so comforted he had closed his eyes and ears on the sounds of Africa and drifted into a deep dreamless sleep.

Gideon's gun woke him again.

The fire had died down but it was still dark, and blinded by sleep Dónal was not at first conscious of where he was. The sight of Gideon Blood crouching on one knee and rapidly reloading his musket brought him back to

Africa with a shock. Even as he watched, Gideon slid the ramrod down the barrel to tap the powder and ball into place, slid it out again, clipped it into its place in the stock and took aim at something out in the darkness. Dónal held his breath and waited for the crash, but after a time Gideon lowered the gun again and heaved a long sigh. He caught sight of Dónal.

'Woke you up, reckon.'

'The gun. Did I hear you shoot?'

'Sure did. They's people comin' up in the bush. Gotta get the fire goin' again.'

Dónal was electrified into action. He scurried around and gathered as much wood as he could find without moving away from Gideon's comforting Kentucky musket, tossed it on the fire and shook the glowing embers into life. Painfully slowly the fire licked the new timbers, glowed, flickered, flamed and burst into light.

'I see 'em. They fixin' to steal our cargo. They goin' to have to do a hell of a lot more'n skulk in the bush.' Gideon's gun was to his shoulder again. Dónal stared at the darkness made blacker by the fact that he had been staring into the fire. In time he made out the scrub trees at the edge of the beach and among them the bright eyes of perhaps a dozen watchers. The watchers were not moving.

'Shoot, Gideon, shoot!'

'Cain't shoot 'em till they do something.' Gideon swore out of the corner of his mouth.

'But who are they, Gideon?'

'Reckon they'd be natives. Hopin' to steal some of this here stuff.' He jerked his thumb at the bales of cotton and the boxes packed with trinkets and guns.

The watchers did not seem to be frightened of the gun. 'Take a shot with your pistol, boy.' Dónal pulled out his pistol and cocked the hammer. Aiming in the general direction of the watching faces he squeezed the trigger. The gun went off, snapping backwards in his hand as it did so, and immediately the faces vanished. Dónal laughed at the effect but Gideon did not move, still staring down the barrel of his musket. Presently Dónal saw the eyes again. They had moved thirty or forty feet to one side but they were still there.

He reloaded his gun. It was something he had never done before and he had to be instructed by Gideon Blood, who never even looked at him. After a while he had cleaned the barrel, spilled in the powder, packed down the wadding, rolled in the ball, packed that in place with wadding and re-cocked the gun.

'Let 'em have it.' Dónal fired on the order and once again saw the faces vanish. Half a minute later they were back where they started. Feverishly Dónal went through the actions of cleaning and loading and packing. Feverishly he re-cocked the gun and without any order fired again. The faces were back moments later. They would not go away. Now Gideon Blood pulled his own pistol from his belt and laid it out on a strip of clean cloth on the sand. Beside it he laid its little bag of shot. Then he took the short cutlass the captain had given him and laid that out beside it. Dónal watched him and then followed suit. He knew Gideon Blood was preparing for an attack.

What were the chances for two of them against the twelve savages, as he now began to think of them?

Perhaps they were cannibals. There were cannibals along this coast. Eli Twiss had told him all about them. What weapons did the savages possess? Lances certainly, perhaps bows and arrows or poison darts. If they attacked, Gideon would fell one with his musket, that was certain. Probably he would bring down another with his pistol. His own pistol must be kept until they got quite close or else he would almost certainly miss. Then, with no time to reload, it would be short cutlasses against lances. Dónal shivered. He threw more timber on the fire and scanned the perimeter of light. The faces were still there watching them and the darkness that they looked out of was alive with the shrieking and wailing of God knew what dreadful animals.

But the night dragged on and there was no screaming charge of savages. The faces seemed to be watching them, making sport of them almost. In the end Dónal concluded that he and Gideon were the object of innocent curiosity, or at worst the only thing standing between the faces and a bit of pilfering. When dawn arrived suddenly in the sky above the shore, the faces had disappeared. Dónal saw them again, flitting like shadows between the distant trees. Then he saw them no more. He wondered now whether he should have behaved differently during the night. Surely if he were at home in Ireland he would have invited them to sit by the fire with him. Why had he and Gideon thrown up their defences and treated them like enemies?

With the dawn came an eerie silence. Dónal rubbed his eyes at the suddenness of the light. Gideon Blood spat tobacco juice into the sand, uncocked his musket and slung the weapon over his arm again.

'Reckon I'll stretch my legs,' he said, yawning, and set off at a rapid walk towards the spot where the watchers had been. Dónal followed and saw that there was a shallow trench like a ditch running along parallel with the shore for about half a mile. He supposed it had once been a river, but it came from nowhere and it led nowhere. It was protected from view by low scrubby bushes. Gideon Blood walked along it some way and came back to Dónal looking thoughtful.

'Might be handy,' he said, though Dónal could not think why.

Two or three hours after dawn Dónal heard what sounded like human voices in the distance. He could not be sure because the high-pitched wailing was just as likely to be coming from one of the animals they had heard during the night, but as it drew closer he could clearly make out two separate sounds – the long drawn out, almost inhuman wail, and the repeated barking and shouting of men.

In time the source of the sound appeared, a thin column of black men, chained to each other at the neck, being driven along by men in European dress, but with dark faces. These men, he was to learn, were the slattees, Africans who collected their countrymen and sold them into slavery. As he watched, the walking column stretched out of the bush and reached the beach, but still the end of the column had not come into view. He tried to count them then, but after a hundred he lost track as the black men drew up on the beach and formed a ragged line. When the end of the long chained column finally came into view Captain Pearson appeared, accompanied by the sailors and a man in elegant white clothes.

Later Dónal learned that this man was the 'factor' who collected the slaves, sometimes using his own men to trap them, sometimes buying them from the warring kingdoms of the interior. The cargo that was drawn up on the beach was what he paid these chiefs with – brass buttons and necklaces, coloured cloth and every kind of trash produced by the booming economy of England. Sometimes indeed he paid them with guns – the guns they had shipped on the *Provident* were intended for no less an eminence than the King of Dahomey, the lord of most of the land they could see, who lived several days' march from the coast. The King of Dahomey was an African, whose people had always made slaves of their enemies captured in battle, and who thought the whole trade a perfect way of dealing with the glut of prisoners that fell to his army now that they had the use of English guns.

Captain Pearson called Dónal over and introduced him to the factor.

'Señor da Silva, may I present a young man who is just beginning to learn this trade, but of whom I expect great things in time. Señor da Silva is a Portuguese gentleman, Dónal. Shake hands.'

Da Silva extended his hand and shook Dónal's warmly. 'What is your name, young man?' he enquired in perfect English.

'I am Dónal Long.'

'Such a pity you could not stay longer and see something of my beautiful Africa, perhaps even meet the king himself. But there is talk that in England the government will abolish our trade and send a squadron of ships to prevent it. Captain Pearson is fearful and wishes to make haste. Perhaps we will meet again.' This last was said to Dónal and the captain together.

'Back next year, for sure,' Captain Pearson replied. 'But for now, Señor, I must take my leave. I must supervise the lading. As you see, my first officer has already ordered the boats.'

'Of course, of course. My men will remove the merchandise.' He waved a gold-ringed hand and a group of men who had been watching and occasionally beating the prisoners handed their whips and weapons to their comrades and began to carry the heavy crates towards the bush. Almost at the same time the boats arrived.

Chaos spread along the beach. Some of the Africans could not be persuaded to enter the boats at all and threw themselves on the sand. No amount of kicking or whipping would move them and eventually they were dragged on board, some of them unconscious, by parties of sailors. Others stepped onto the boats with a quiet dignity that amazed Dónal. These men stared over their shoulders at their homeland as the boats pulled out and their eyes seemed to have the most painful loneliness in them, so that Dónal was reminded of his own native land. He was filled with pity for them but in the brutal atmosphere of the beach he realised that no pleading would have any effect.

As the afternoon wore on, the beach gradually emptied until finally all that was left was a small mound of merchandise and a boat with four oarsmen, Captain Pearson, Gideon Blood and Dónal. Da Silva had made his goodbyes earlier and just for the moment none of his men was nearby.

'Look lively there, men,' the captain hissed. 'We'll ship the last of the cargo. Waste not want not, as I always say.'

'But that's stealing, Captain. You're breaking your bargain with da Silva!' Dónal was surprised at himself. What did he care about da Silva and his guns? Captain Pearson looked black but said nothing. The men grinned and began dragging the crates towards the boat, delighted to be cheating the factor out of some of his bargain. They had loaded four of the eight remaining crates when they heard a shout and saw one of da Silva's men running towards the trees.

'Quick!' the captain said, fear in his voice now. 'Shove off there! Leave the rest!'

But they had forgotten that the boat would have to be dragged down to the water with the weight of the merchandise in it, and that it would then have to be launched into the surf. They put their shoulders to the gunwale and pushed for their lives. Dónal felt the rush of cold water underfoot and felt the boat lift slightly on the tide. Then there were shots and he heard one of the sailors cry out. When he looked up he saw the man in front of him bleeding at the shoulder.

The boat was afloat and surging furiously in the waves. Some of the sailors were already pulling on the oars. Dónal tried to scramble aboard.

'No room,' the captain shouted, pushing Dónal back. 'Gideon Blood and the boy stay here. We'll come back with a lighter boat!'

Gideon Blood had already turned and unslung his

musket. Dónal saw him fire and heard a cry from the top of the beach. 'Quick, boy! The trench.'

Dónal knew immediately what he meant and sprinted for the place where the faces had been last night. As he fell into its shelter he pulled out the pistol and cocked it. He heard Gideon's gun fire again lower down, nearer the water, and heard the short cry of a man going down. Then he heard heavy footsteps and the sound of the men in the boat discharging their guns. He turned towards the sound and barely stopped himself from firing into Gideon Blood's stomach as he dropped into the trench.

Gideon reloaded furiously while Dónal kept watch along the tree line.

'They're gone, Gideon. I can't see anyone.'

'They'll be back. I dropped two of them.'

'Wounded?'

'This gun don't wound. They'll be dead.'

Once again they laid out their weapons where they could make best use of them and settled down to wait. The trench gave them a slight advantage. Firstly they had the only cover on the beach. Secondly they had a steady rest for their weapons and perhaps an element of surprise since they could move along the trench a considerable distance without being seen.

'Somethin' a-rustling yonder,' Gideon said, indicating the direction with a nod of his head. Hardly had he spoken when four men appeared. They had not seen Dónal and Gideon in their trench, and were looking fixedly at the remaining crates on the beach.

They think we're hiding behind the crates, Dónal thought. They began to advance at an angle, obviously trying to get a better shot at the crates. Each of them had one of the new English guns.

'They keep a-comin' they goin' to see us, boy. Gotta shoot first. You take the small fella. Wait till they close enough to get a good shot.' Gideon picked up his pistol and they both waited.

The time seemed to stretch out for Dónal. The men moved slowly, a few paces at a time, their eyes fixed on the crates. Soon, he knew, they would see the side of the crates that had been hidden when they first came in view and then they would know that no sailors crouched behind them. That would be the vital moment. Dónal and Gideon must fire then and hope to hit, and if they did not, the men would fall back and track them down, or go for their fellows to reinforce the attack.

At length Dónal saw Gideon place the pistol on top of the bank of earth they were leaning on. 'Ready, boy? Aim low, for his knees. The gun'll jump up.'

Dónal did as he was bid and took careful aim at the man's knees, waiting for the word from Gideon. When it came he felt the gun kick in his hand, saw its smoke cloud the target for a moment and then he saw the man fall backwards clutching his chest. How the gun, which had been aimed at the knees, had placed its ball in the man's chest was beyond Dónal's understanding. Dónal saw the man get painfully to his knees and crawl away into the bush. Gideon had fired too, and hit, and they could hear a man groaning from the shot, but the other two were running for the woods, completely taken by surprise. Gideon placed his musket on the earth, took a slow aim and shot one of the retreating men square in the back.

Dónal saw the shot strike, a sudden flowering of blood, and the body jerked forward as though caught by a powerful wind. Then the man vanished from sight.

Now all they could hear was the groaning of the man wounded by Gideon's pistol. The sound reminded Dónal that for the first time in his life he had fired a gun at another human being. Immediately he felt his gorge rise and he stumbled a few feet and was sick into the coarse grass. When he turned, wiping his lips, Gideon was laughing quietly.

'Took me like that the first man I killed,' he said. 'Wouldn't be natural elseways.'

At that moment a gun in the ship began firing and they heard the ball crashing into the trees a long way off. Gideon laughed again. 'Well, they must be goin' to pick us up after all, boy.' For the first time Dónal realised that Gideon had not expected to be picked up. Sure enough, there was a boat making its way through the surf, and three of the four starboard guns were firing. He saw their smoke and heard the balls passing overhead as he re-loaded his own pistol. The firing was ragged and slow, not like the disciplined naval firing that he had grown used to in his days on the *Leander*, but effective just the same. With the added risk of Gideon's deadly accurate musket fire, the slattees would not be likely to attack now. Soon the boat was at the edge of the water. Dónal saw the sailors jump out and immediately make for the crates. With a start he realised that they had come back for the cargo, not for them.

'Quick, Gideon. They came for the crates. We have to get down to the boat!' He jumped up and started to run and in a moment Gideon was behind him. Suddenly the sailors ahead of them dropped their crates, reached into the boat and pulled out muskets. With mounting horror Dónal saw them shoulder and cock the weapons and take aim, it seemed, directly at him. He saw them fire and heard the balls whistle by without hitting him. A shout from Gideon Blood made him look round and he saw six or seven of the factor's men rushing after them, swords swinging over their heads. At the same time he heard their shouts, war cries to his ears, and wondered that he had not heard it before. The sailors were frantically tossing the crates into the boat and shoving off into the surf.

Dónal saw Gideon Blood stop and he stopped too. Gideon dropped on one knee and fired and Dónal saw one of their pursuers throw up his arms and fall backwards. Then they were both running again. They reached the boat as the sailors were pulling her out through the surf, and they had to launch themselves bodily into her. Not one of the sailors paused to lend them a hand.

No sooner had Dónal picked himself up from the bottom of the boat than the pursuers were on top of them, wading waist deep into the exploding surf. In a hectic minute Dónal fired his pistol at point blank range, realised he had missed, but saw his target drop his sword and cover his eyes, blasted by the smoke and flame. He saw a sword smash one of the oars, and the sailor, whose oar it was, pushing at his attacker with what was left of it. Gideon's pistol went off near Dónal's ear as he was feeling in the bottom of the boat for his cutlass. There were groans and cries and shouts and then they were into deeper water. The attackers were retreating, two of them carrying a wounded man between them. Dónal could see the man he had blinded, desperately scooping water onto his face. Then he saw that the sailor nearest him had fallen dead over his oar, his head almost severed. Another had a deep gash in the arm. Gideon Blood was bleeding from a wound on his face. But they were clear. At least they would not fall into the hands of the factor who might make slaves of them, or turn them over to some cannibal tribe as payment for some favour or other. Certainly, in the slave factor's eyes they must deserve worse, cheating him of his merchandise. Dónal had time to wonder about the mind of Captain Pearson, who had risked leaving Dónal and Gideon Blood behind, all for a few crates of guns.

4

FEEDING THE SHARKS

Mr Munro was explaining the workings of the slave trade to Dónal. 'Bristol and Liverpool in England. They are the slave capitals of the world. The merchants of those towns have grown rich and fat. I have heard that these cities alone have two thousand ships engaged upon the trade. And I have heard it said that six millions of savages have been brought out of Africa in the last century.'

Dónal was listening intently. 'But surely, sir, you cannot approve it? Stealing these human beings from their homes. And then to take them to a country they know nothing of, there to be sold at auction to the highest bidder, as I have heard it said. Surely no Christian could approve it!'

Mr Munro looked at Dónal with pity. 'Firstly, you must remember, young man, that these savages live in the utmost ignorance of God. They are pagans, pagans of the worst kind, worshipping false gods and eating of human flesh into the bargain. I declare, it is a kindness to bring them out of it. To win them home for God. They will be baptised by their new masters and live as Christians from that day on, with a sure and certain hope of salvation. Secondly, you must remember that the wealth of nations is founded upon slavery. It is now, and it always was. I remember noting where the Latin writer Plutarch mentions that one hundred and fifty thousands of slaves were sold in a single market in Rome in one year. The Greeks had slaves. The Hebrews were slaves in Egypt even. "All their service, wherein they made them serve, was with rigour" as the good book saith. In turn, after their deliverance into the promised land, the Hebrews themselves owned slaves – and our Lord Jesus Christ was a Hebrew.' Mr Munro looked piercingly at Dónal. On a previous occasion he had replied in harsh words when Dónal had declared that Jesus Christ would never have approved of slavery. But now Dónal held his tongue, wanting nothing so much as an end to all these explanations.

'Not only do I approve it, young man, not only does the wealth of nations require it, but God himself approves it in Holy Writ.'

Overwhelmed by all this learned argument, Dónal could not think of a single word to say to dispute with the second mate. He sat in glum silence, conscious of the authority with which Mr Munro spoke, but still obstinately believing that no man had the right to enslave another. But now Mr Munro was talking about the profits of the trade.

'Four hundred slaves, young man, prime flesh!' Dónal shuddered. He had come to hate the word 'flesh'. 'Before the law of 1788 we could pack as many of them as we liked into the hold. Now we are only permitted four hundred and fifty. I mind the time a ship of this size would hold six hundred blackbirds. That is why we are called "tight-packers", because we pack 'em tight.' Mr Munro smiled at the phrase.

'But we do have four hundred of them. That is something. Each fetching thirty-five or perhaps forty-five pounds on the block in Jamaica! More than twenty thousand pounds! A vast profit. And the beauty of it, you see, is that most of it *is* profit. Think but this: we brought a cargo of our New England rum to Cork. We sold it at the usual tidy profit. We half paid for the voyage in that transaction alone. Then we spent a small amount of our profit again in buying the guns and the trash to barter with da Silva. Another small portion of our moneys went to him, in gold to make up the difference. Now we sail for Jamaica to make our fortune. For sure, we may not come out with twenty thousand pounds; but consider, young man, that we will carry a cargo of cane sugar and molasses from Jamaica to New England so that the industrious New Englanders can again make their rum. We will make a handsome profit on that part too.'

Dónal said something about profiting by another man's misery and Mr Munro flared up. 'The ways of the wicked, young man! Drunkenness is a punishment on the wicked! The wages of sin is death, death of the soul! The Lord punishes the idle of this world with poverty. Wealth is a blessing that must not be refused.'

Eight bells sounded through the ship and Mr Munro had to go on deck for his watch. Dónal never felt so happy to be relieved of the company of another person. He got up and drew breath through an open port, hoping to clear his head of Mr Munro's terrible teachings.

When he told all this to his uncle he was surprised that Michael Long seemed to agree with a lot of it. 'The black man is below us in station,' he told Dónal. 'He is a blackguard and a good-for-nothing. Look at all those . . . *things* in the hold. Are they men and women? They are not.'

'Why?' Dónal replied, furious at his uncle's bigotry. 'Do they drink too much and beat their children with belts the way you did me?' His uncle snarled and grabbed at his arm but Dónal squirmed out of his grasp and launched himself into the rigging. In three steps he was out of his uncle's reach. 'Don't you ever lay a hand on me again, Michael Long, or I'll pistol you!' he hissed. Michael Long looked into Dónal's eyes for a moment then turned on his heel and walked away.

What Mr Munro had left out of his calculations was what Captain Pearson continually referred to as 'our accursed twenty per cent'. This twenty per cent was what the officers expected to lose in the course of the Middle Passage. One in every five of the Africans would die, as surely as the winds would eventually blow. One in five was, according to Captain Pearson, what had to be expected. 'God send we lose no more,' he prayed.

The dying had started a few days out of Benin. The winds were light, the air hot. The equatorial stillness was poisoning the sky and the sea, and it was poisoning the ship itself. Although they were making for Porto-Novo to take on food and water, there was little hope of reaching it in the present conditions. The Africans were unaccus-

tomed to the motion of the ship, the crowded conditions
and the bad food. Vomiting and diarrhoea had set in.
Chained in a space no bigger than a child's cot, unable
to stand up or lie down, to clean themselves or avoid their
neighbours, the Africans were confined like animals. No,
not like any animals Dónal had ever seen or heard of. No
one would treat a dog, or even a pig, the way the slaves
were treated.

In these conditions disease was quick to spread. The
sailors knew the names of all the diseases that could
strike. River blindness, yellow jack, the bloody flux,
malaria, dysentery . . . They named them constantly to
Dónal, always glancing aloft as they did so to see if the
blessed wind was blowing yet. The wind would waft them
into Porto-Novo where they would take on stores. Then
it would drive them across the Atlantic, and the fresh air
and the quick voyage would preserve them from the evils
that waited on their trade.

Eli Twiss told him of the *Leon*. She was a slaver in
these waters. A French ship spied her, foresails aback,
lying to, pretty rough. As the French ship closed her the
helmsman saw that every man-jack aboard was blind. All
those whitened sightless eyes staring out of the starving
faces. He sheered off and left them to die. Why? Because
every man aboard the French ship was blind too, barring
the helmsman. He brought her safely in and lived to tell
the tale.

Whole ships' companies had died of the yellow jack,
a terrible fever that swept through slave ships sometimes.
In some ships if a man, white or black, sailor or slave,
was seen with it, he would be put over the side directly,

alive or dead, and the sharks could have him.

Dónal had noticed the huge increase in the numbers of sharks that followed the boat.

'They always follows the slavers! They's good bait in the slave carcasses. Them boys know how to fill their bellies!' Eli Twiss cackled with laughter at his joke, but Dónal noticed that none of the sailors, Eli Twiss included, liked the following sharks. They had a superstitious dread of them in fact. Their eyes showed it when they looked at the lines of coursing fins.

Ever since he and Gideon Blood had rejoined the ship he had noticed the change that had come over everyone. There was no joking now, no pranks, no songs or story-telling unless it were stories of the dangers they faced in what they called the Middle Passage, the voyage from Africa to the West Indies. Eli Twiss seemed to know them all. Joe Quane was full of gloom and hardly spoke to Gideon, his old friend. Dónal learned from another sailor that Quane felt bad about the way Gideon had been left behind ashore to hold off the attackers, and he blamed Captain Pearson, who in Joe's opinion was happy to leave Gideon and Dónal to die provided he could cheat the slave factor of some little bit of the cargo. Equally, Gideon was sunk in silence. Never one to speak too much, he never uttered a word now.

The officers were altered too. Mr Munro had seemed to be a fair and decent officer to Dónal. Now his lack of feeling was evident in almost every word he spoke. He believed heartily in the slave system, as heartily as the most uneducated sailor, perhaps more so. He could produce facts and phrases from the Bible and from ancient writers to support his viewpoint. He treated the slaves in a much crueller fashion than the other officers did. When they came on deck for their twenty minutes of exercise he would read sections of the Bible to them, and if they were sick or inattentive he would order the bosun to wake them up with a blow of his rope-end. As the days went on, the Africans became weaker and more subdued, and this seemed to please him. It was as though they were learning to listen, he frequently told Dónal.

Mr Burgess was drunk when Dónal came aboard after the fight. He seemed to have been drinking heavily ever since and was rarely completely sober. Captain Pearson kept to his quarterdeck and only intervened in the running of the ship to order that hoses be used to wash the slave decks whenever the smell reached him.

That smell poisoned everything and everyone as the days wore on. It was the smell of sickness, death and decay. But worst of all was the other smell that Dónal thought he could detect wherever he went. The air was polluted by it and it polluted the heart of every seaman aboard. Dónal came to recognise it as the smell of evil – the evil that men do to others. It was the smell of Dónal's disgrace.

While Dónal and Gideon Blood had been waiting on shore for the slaves to arrive, Eli Twiss had transformed the hold of an innocent merchant ship into the deadly prison of more than four hundred Africans. Where before there was a single large hold, like a huge room, now there were three flimsy decks. Each deck was no more than two and a half feet from the one above it. It was possible to crawl along between the decks, or it would have been if every single inch had not been taken up with slaves, the frightened, miserable, homesick, suffering, dying human beings that the sailors called by various names – 'black-birds', 'flesh', 'trade', 'blackamoors' and a dozen other terms designed to make them seem less than human, to make it possible for Dónal's shipmates to keep them chained by the neck to the timbers of the slave decks. Down there the air was scarcely breathable, and already disease had started. There was no ship's surgeon because Captain Pearson had decided to save his salary. Instead Burgess or Munro went down every evening to examine the health of the slaves.

One evening Dónal came on Mr Burgess standing in the companion. He was so still that Dónal wondered if he was sick himself and touched him on the shoulder to ask if he was well. The mate swung round and glared at Dónal and his eyes looked blank, as if he could not see him. Dónal could smell the cloud of brandy fumes that always enveloped the mate now and he noticed that there were the marks of tears on the man's face. Burgess stared at him for a moment without recognition, then, recollecting himself, he took Dónal gently by the elbow and led him into his cabin.

'Close the door, Dónal boy,' he said.

'Are you well, sir? You startled me there.'

'I ain't well and that's the truth. I fear I have slave fever!' Dónal was shocked. It was a disease that he had not heard the sailors mention and surely that meant it was the worst of all.

'Is it fatal, sir? Will I call in the captain?'

The mate laughed. 'I mean by that, Dónal, that I cannot

complete this voyage. I have done it before, you see. Once before. Cap'n Pearson and me. It was terrible. A mighty nightmare of a voyage. I cannot do it again.' He sat down heavily on the edge of his sea-berth. 'I know you think the worse of me, boy. You have seen me drive the men and curse at them. I know you fear me and hate me, but I must tell you this, as bad as I am I cannot bear this dreadful trade another day.'

Dónal felt a rush of pity for the first mate. 'Sir, we must make the best of it. I doubt not we will find a way.'

The mate looked up with a sheepish kind of hope in his face. 'A way?'

'We are bound for Porto-Novo. We could jump ship.'

The mate's face darkened again. 'It ain't possible. We'd be deserters and Porto-Novo is too small to hide us. Pearson would catch us and flog us, or turn us over to the authorities who might hang us.'

Dónal was stunned. 'This is not a navy ship. We cannot be hanged for leaving.'

Wearily the mate explained. 'We signed on for the voyage, boy. You and me. And Porto-Novo is a slave town, remember. The merchants there depend on the trade. There's not a one of them but would pay to have our throats slit, just to discourage others from doing the same. And the blasted Portuguese would probably hang us. The place is run by them.'

He stared glumly at his feet. 'I was tricked, you know. Cap'n Pearson told me it was over to Ireland and back. I'm to sit for my master's ticket next April. Then I will captain my own ship. If I desert now I will never make it.'

Desperate though Mr Burgess was, Dónal was glad because he knew now that he had at least one ally on board. He did not count his uncle because Michael Long spoke of the Africans in the same way as the rest of the men. Dónal found it harder to talk to him now than he had ever done. Besides, he had long ago learned that the man was not to be trusted.

A week of drifting, with barely enough wind to fill the sails, and the first deaths occurred. Dónal was awakened from an uneasy sleep by the sound of a splash. He hurried on deck and saw two men in the waist of the ship slinging a bundle over the side. They were supervised by Mr Munro and watched from the quarterdeck by Captain Pearson. Two more sailors appeared through the grating of the slave deck, and this time the bundle had arms and legs which dangled limply out from the sheet of sailcloth they were carrying. This bundle went over the side too, and with a sickening shock Dónal realised that the sharks were at last being rewarded for their loyalty.

5
CAPTAIN PEARSON'S PIPE

They stood out to sea at last, Porto-Novo behind them,
the broad Atlantic and the steady trade winds ahead. They
had lost eleven slaves in the doldrums where they had
lain for two weeks. Then the breeze had set in that carried
them up to Porto-Novo, where they had taken on water
and fresh vegetables, fruit and meat. Captain Pearson
rubbed his hands together and declared that he was well
pleased with their good luck. Eleven slaves was a small
loss. God send they would catch the trade winds soon and
make a fast passage to the West Indies. One sailor
deserted in Porto-Novo and was taken up by the authorities and handed back to Captain Pearson for punishment,
a punishment that turned out to be no more than a day
in the foretop where the sun beat down on him. Captain
Pearson was in a benevolent mood as they left the land
behind. The deck heeled beneath him, the wind served for
America, he was going home and, barring accidents, calms
or catastrophic storms, he would be a rich man in a very
short space of time.

The *Provident* settled back into her daily routine. The men sang their songs, 'The Congo River' a particular favourite with them now. The four-hour watches were marked out by the striking of a bell every half hour. And then there were the two dogwatches in the afternoon, two hours each. Sailors stood their watch and went below to sleep or lounged about the deck. The northeast trade winds blew steadily and the days were bright, with only small white clouds to set off the continuous blue. Dónal marvelled at this wonderful sailing, the ship rolling on her way with never a hand to her sails for hours on end, the weather fine, the sky and sea an equal blue, the air warm. It would have been the most perfect time of his life if his conscience did not keep him awake at night wondering how he could have found himself on this ship of all ships; if it were not for the thought of the suffering below decks and the rising stench that filled the ship.

Dónal knew by now that the men and women were chained below deck 'two by two', the right wrist and ankle of one being shackled to the left wrist and ankle of another. Some were chained by the neck to the planks. The men were lying in a space six feet long by sixteen inches wide. The women were allotted a space five feet ten inches long by twelve inches wide. The spaces were so narrow they could not lie on their backs. The boards they lay on were unplaned and rough, and in many cases the captives' elbows were rubbed raw and bleeding.

Dónal racked his brains for a way out but could find none. Mr Burgess had been right about Porto-Novo – there was no escaping there. It was a miserable place, visited almost entirely by slaving ships. Even if he had succeeded in escaping he would have had to ship aboard another vessel equally bad, or perhaps worse.

He watched the slaves closely as they were brought on deck for their exercise every day, wondering whether he could somehow free them from their chains, and whether then they might be got to work the ship back towards Africa. But they had been so long confined below decks that by now they could not straighten their backs. They were pitifully thin and wasted, though he was impressed by their courage. He did not think that he could preserve what little dignity he had in such circumstances.

They were ten days out when he became aware that Mr Munro was quietly murdering the weaker slaves.

He continued to meet his uncle each night as before, though later now because the huge number of additional mouths to feed kept the big copper vats that his uncle cooked in busy almost all day and late into the evening. Michael Long had sunk into the same mood as the others on board and he made very poor company for Dónal. They never discussed the slave trade again.

One evening after they had parted, his uncle returning to the galley where he slept on a narrow plank, Dónal lingered in the warm night air, wondering whether he should once again resume his practice of sleeping on deck. He watched the sea course by and fell to remembering his childhood, when he often went out on moonlit nights to fish with his father on the *Ellen Brice*, those happy days when all he wanted from life was to be out on the water talking with his father and his crew, hauling their nets, gutting the fish. All that hard labour seemed to him now to be the softest play imaginable. Then he thought about his friends and neighbours at home and wondered how they were, and whether the terrible trouble of the 1798 rising had died down yet.

He was startled out of his thoughts by the sound of voices, and instinctively stepped into the shadows of the quarterdeck bulkhead. He saw one of the gratings of the slave deck thrown back and the head and shoulders of Mr Munro emerge through the opening. The second mate paused for a moment and spoke to someone below, then he climbed out completely. Dónal could see he had a pistol in his right hand. Two men emerged after him, carrying an African between them. The African was so thin and lifeless that Dónal assumed he was dead until he heard the man speak. His voice was as clear and strong as his body was lifeless. What he said Dónal never knew, because it was in the language of his country, but he saw Mr Munro reverse the pistol and strike the man in the face with the butt. After that the man made no further protest.

Munro strode to the leeward bulwark and motioned the others to bring their burden along. Then they stood by the side and counted one, two, three, swinging the man each time, until on the count of three they released their hold and the man went over the side.

Dónal heard the splash, and immediately, instinctively shouted, 'Man overboard!'

The cry of 'man overboard' on a ship is the one cry likely to bring the whole crew on deck almost instantly, and before Munro and his men had time to react, the off-watch crew was spilling up from below and men were coming out of the shadows along the deck where they had been sleeping, ready for a call to duty. In a matter of moments they were getting a boat ready to launch, climbing out on the chainplates, staring astern and generally creating a fuss.

Dónal stepped from the shadows then, and Munro and his men saw him. In the full moonlight Dónal felt frail and exposed, and he saw by the same light that one of the men was Joe Quane.

'On deck there, where away?' The shout came from the quarterdeck. Burgess and Captain Pearson were up, the captain still in his nightshirt.

'I heard a splash, sir.' An angry growl from the captain. Burgess clenched his fists. From past experience Dónal knew the mate could fly into a temper with less provocation than this.

A voice from the chainplates. 'Dead astern! A man in the water!'

All eyes focused on the ship's wake where the shape of the lost man was clearly visible. Captain Pearson responded instantly. 'Launch your boat! Mr Burgess, we shall have to bring up. All hands stand by to heave to. Davit tackles!'

In the frenzy of activity that followed, Munro and Quane and the other man melted into the crowd.

The ship came round slowly, bringing up in the eye of the wind with all sails shivering. It was a long drawn out process and one that required all hands on deck. In the meantime the boat had pulled away for the place where the man had last been seen. When the ship was safely lying to in the waves the bosun began to call the names of the crew to see who was missing. This was the moment Dónal was dreading. One by one the sailors answered to the muster roll and one by one they crossed their names off the bosun's mental list of who might have gone overboard. Finally, the bosun knew that no one was gone. Not one member of the crew was absent.

Now a dreadful, superstitious silence settled over the deck. What had the cabin boy heard? Who or what was that human shape in the moonlit water? All sorts of rumours began to pass among the waiting hands. It was a drowned sailor, come to haunt the ship. It was a mermaid, certain to mean bad luck. It was a sea serpent that would swallow the ship. When the boat returned after two hours of searching, not having found a thing, each man was certain that his own fear was the right one. Superstition had taken hold of the sailors' minds.

The following morning Dónal was called to account for his warning shout. The captain and Mr Burgess were waiting for him in the captain's cabin, but on the way there Dónal bumped into Joe Quane.

'Good morning, Dónal,' Quane said. He managed to make the greeting sound menacing. 'I've something to show you.' He reached a hand into the breast of his shirt and when it came out again Dónal saw that it held a long, slender knife with an edge on both sides. 'This ain't a sailor's knife, boy. This here's the knife of a cut-throat. It does very well for the cutting out of tongues and such.' He slipped the knife back into the shirt and grinned at Dónal. 'Be sure and tell the truth now,' and he was gone.

Both the captain and the mate had grave, intense looks on their faces. They sat behind the captain's table and motioned Dónal to stand in front of them. Then the captain lectured him for five minutes on the seriousness of the 'man overboard' cry. How it brought all hands on deck. How every man feared that his best friend might be the one who was gone. How it was the duty of the captain to bring the ship up all standing and how tricky, even dangerous, that manoeuvre was. How a false warning might endanger the lifeboat's crew, the ship herself even, and all aboard her. And so on. Dónal knew all of this and did not need to be told. He withstood the lecture as best he could, turning over in his mind again and again how best he might make clear to the captain and the mate what had happened, without at the same time drawing Joe Quane's deadly blade down on him. At length the captain began the questioning.

'You called man overboard last night, Dónal Long.'

'I did, sir.'

'Describe how you came to make that call, if you please.'

Dónal picked his words with care. 'I was coming on deck, sir, for my customary evening walk to catch the night air and watch the waves pass in the moonlight. It reminds me of my childhood on my father's boat, you see.'

They nodded impatiently. 'Get on with it, boy!'

'Yes, sir. Well, as I came through the companion I heard voices and then a splash. I know that splash, sir. It is the splash of a person falling into the sea. I have heard it so often since you began to throw the dead – ' he almost choked on the word, 'the dead blackamoors over the side. However I knew that this throwing over of the dead occurs only in the morning, for I have seen it as well as heard it. Therefore, I stepped out immediately and called out.

It was then that I saw Mr Munro and Joe Quane and the other man whose face I did not see. They were looking over the side as though they had heard it too. I make no doubt they would have called out if I had not done so first.'

'There was no man overboard, sir. You are impertinent.'

'On the contrary, sir, I believe every man aboard clearly saw the shape of a man in our wake. I was not mistaken. I am certain of it.'

Burgess spoke now. 'You are very certain of yourself. We will call Mr Munro and Joe Quane. Unless they spin the same yarn you will be flogged.'

Joe Quane was standing outside the cabin when Dónal came out, and if looks could kill, Dónal would have died on the spot. But Dónal was expecting it and knew by it that Quane must have heard his evidence. He was sure now that he and Munro would tell the same story.

Up on the quarterdeck it was not difficult to overhear Munro's evidence. There was a case-light there, a window into the cabin, and its panes were open to let in as much air as possible. Dónal stationed himself beside that and heard Mr Munro state that he and Joe Quane and Thomas Benting were on deck seeing to a grating which had come loose during the day. They heard a splash, rushed to the side and then heard the cabin boy give the alarm. They saw nothing, other than what everyone else saw.

Joe Quane and Thomas Benting said the same thing a few minutes later. Then Dónal was called back in.

'I am entering it in the log as a false alarm, boy. I reckon that's the best thing I can do.' The captain was already writing but Burgess looked straight at Dónal and for the first time in a long while Dónal thought that those eyes looked clear and sober. The captain, on the other hand, was grey-faced and cloudy-eyed, looking almost asleep, and his voice came thick and slow. He wiped his hand across his eyes continually as though a light web had fallen across them, or as though he were brushing aside a muslin curtain. There was none of the usual trim air of command about him, and Dónal remembered that for the past week he had sent his food back almost untouched. Dónal had supposed the heat was too much for him and had taken away his appetite. Now Dónal thought he looked ill, his face florid and sweaty, his eyes puffed up. Dónal hoped he was not coming down with the yellow jack or the flux or some other dreadful scourge such as he was continually hearing about.

'I will have a word with the boy, Cap'n, and lay out his duties for him. I'll make sure it don't happen again.'

'Very good, Mr Burgess. Make it so.' The captain waved a hand at the two of them by way of dismissal.

As they made their way back on deck, Mr Burgess said, 'I'd appreciate a word or two later, boy. To lay out your duties for you.' Then in a half-whisper he added, 'They're murdering the weaker slaves, am I right?' Dónal nodded. 'We'll strike their colours for them, boy. Never fear. We might do something yet. Come down to my cabin at six bells in the first watch. Come quickly.'

Since they had come into the tropic seas Captain Pearson had stopped appearing unexpectedly on the quarterdeck. On the voyage south from Ireland no sailor knew when to expect 'the old man' as they called him. He might be standing there on deck in his nightshirt at midnight, appearing as if by magic to watch the working of the ship. But now he kept his cabin from the first watch on. Dónal served him his dinner during the second dogwatch, that is to say between six and eight in the evening, land-time. The captain then closed his cabin door, giving strict orders that he was not to be disturbed unless there were an emergency.

Sharply at six bells Dónal knocked on Mr Burgess's cabin door. It was opened immediately and, laying his finger to his lips to indicate silence, Mr Burgess led him aft to the captain's cabin. He opened the door slowly and quietly and entered with a step that surprised Dónal by its lightness. At a glance Dónal took in the room he had come to know so well – the dining table now trim and swept clean, the chairs, the books, the chart table and its navigation instruments, and the captain, thrown on his berth as he had seen him on the night he found out they were heading for the Bight of Benin.

But Mr Burgess pointed to a complicated arrangement of pipe and tube lying on the floor beside the captain's cot. Dónal had never seen it before, although he was convinced he knew everything in this room.

'It's a hookah,' the mate whispered, and seeing Dónal's blank look he added, 'Opium. That's an opium pipe. A hubble-bubble they call it, or a hookah.'

Dónal still did not understand and the mate led him back the way they came. Standing outside the captain's door, Mr Burgess explained the workings of the drug opium to Dónal, who had never heard of such things in Ireland. Dónal learned how the drug gave an uneasy, dream-filled sleep, and relief from pain and suffering, how it took hold of the body and mind so that the smoker could not give it up, how it caused loss of appetite and weakness in the smoker. How it gave rise to nightmares after a time, waking or sleeping, and caused terrible pains if the pipe could not be had. How Mr Burgess had seen the dreaded drug kill friends at sea.

'He had a little with him all along but he bought a good store of it in Porto-Novo from an Indian merchant there. He has been an opium-eater for five or six years now, since he made a voyage to the Yellow River in China. He has taken to it very badly this time.'

'But we are in the hands of a drunkard, so,' Dónal said. 'It is as if he were habitually drunk.'

Mr Burgess flinched at the reference to drunkenness. 'And I have not been too good that way. But I am sober now.' He heaved a deep sigh. 'Nathaniel Pearson is my friend, Dónal, and a good friend he has been to me in his time. But he's wrong-shipped now. It grieves me to say so, but he is no longer fit to command.' He looked downcast for a moment, then his eyes began to gleam. 'But looky here, this pipe-smoking may be the saving of us, boy. It may allow me to seize the ship.'

Dónal's heart skipped a beat. 'Seize the ship? Is it not mutiny? Will we be hanged for it?'

The mate chuckled. 'Your time in the navy has given you a royal fear of the gallows, I see. But no. Under sea law, an officer may seize the ship if his cap'n is unable to fulfil his duties. Through sickness, for example. Or insanity. Or habitual drunkenness. Opium-eating would fit the bill too.' Dónal saw that sweat stood out on the mate's forehead in broad beads and that there was a feverish glare in his eyes. 'We would need witnesses. There would be a court of enquiry.'

Dónal knew what he was asking. 'I'll be your witness, sir. With a heart and a half.'

'Good. But we will need others too. Your uncle perhaps?'

Dónal shook his head. 'Never trust him, sir. He will betray you.'

'If there were one or two others . . . '

Dónal mentioned Gideon Blood.

'Why Gideon would do nicely if you could bring him round.'

'I believe I can,' Dónal said, thinking that killer though Gideon Blood was, he had no taste for this inhumanity that passed for 'trade'.

'We will have to get Munro out of the way and that ain't so easy. That's where your evidence comes in. Perhaps we can catch him in the act. We'll lay to and watch out for him. Murder is murder, on the high seas just as much as in Boston. I can clap him in irons for that. A murderer for a second mate and an opium-eating captain! No court could say but we did well to seize the ship then!'

'But why does he do it? Mr Munro, I mean. Why does he kill them?'

'Economy, Dónal boy. The weak ones eat the food of the strong ones and they spread disease, and they ain't going to fetch much at the auction block. It's cheaper to feed them to the sharks!'

6
—

A Barbary Pirate

'Sail ho! Hull down. Astern.' The cry from the lookout brought all hands to the rails staring into the dawn light. Nothing could be seen from that level however; the lookout was fifty feet higher in his station on the mainmast. Mr Burgess climbed to the same height with his brass telescope and sat there for some time studying the new arrival. When he came down he looked puzzled. He and Munro paced the quarterdeck – the captain was still abed and had not been roused by the lookout's cry.

'She's like a naval vessel. Maybe a sloop of war. A single decker. Gunports open. But her sails are filthy and badly trimmed. She looks slovenly.' Dónal knew what he was saying. No ship of any navy in the world could be described in those terms. Battle damaged, perhaps. Sails full of holes. Masts shot away. Hull shattered and leaking. But no sooner would the battle be over than the men would be set to cleaning up, making all good again. This slovenly sloop could not be a navy ship.

'She's coming up on us. She'll overhaul us before long.'

Mr Munro pursed his lips. 'A Barbary?'

'Could be. A bit too far afield for them I would have thought.'

'They go very far afield now. They're a plague to the trade routes, seizing merchantmen and ransoming and slaving everywhere. It's got so bad that when I was last in Boston I heard tell of a squadron being raised to cut them out. The *Constitution* is named for it. They say they will bombard Tripoli to drive them out. Aye, she could be a Barbary pirate.'

The telescopes were in use again, both men staring grimly into the eyepiece.

'Well,' said Mr Burgess, 'laden as we are we'll have to make a run for it. All sail, Mr Munro. All possible sail.'

Mr Munro strode down into the waist shouting, 'All hands to make sail.'

'Gun crews to stand to their guns once we have sail up,' Mr Burgess shouted. 'Load number three gun on each side with case.'

Dónal shivered at the word 'case'. A charge of case-shot was used to clear a deck of men. The gun would be loaded with powder first, then the wadding that held the powder in place. Then came the case-shot – though on a ship like this it would not be shot at all, just nails and bits of metal or stone. The shot would spread out and pepper anything in its way. A whole deck could be swept clean by a broadside of case-shot, men going down in agony, riddled with metal, eyes lost, rusted nails in the stomach. Sure enough, as the guns were being prepared for action Dónal saw Eli Twiss coming along the deck with a bucket of nails and scraps of metal.

'Long, I believe you have served as a powder monkey?'
Mr Munro looked grim.

'I have, sir.'

'That being the case you can do the same duty here.
Twiss will show you where the powder is kept.'

The ship had crowded on sail, and a glance at the
chasing ship convinced Dónal that they would escape her.
He went below a little happier that they might not have
to face battle at all. Nevertheless he set about his work
with a will, serving the powder into packets and stowing
them where he could get at them quickly in the event of
an attack. When he emerged on deck again the first thing
he did was glance astern at the chaser. She was still there,
closer now, so close that he could make out the stained
sails. So he had been wrong; they would have to fight after
all. All day they ran as best they could but the slovenly
pirate ship kept pace and even drew closer. By evening
the situation was desperate.

Mr Burgess called Dónal to the quarterdeck. 'It'll be
dark in half an hour. Tell Eli Twiss I want him.'

Eli Twiss was sitting in his carpenter's shop, calmly
smoking a pipe. 'Eli, I think it will come to a battle.' Eli
winked without ceasing to smoke. 'They think she might
be a pirate ship,' Dónal continued.

Eli took the pipe from his mouth and pointed the stem
at Dónal. 'What you want disturbing my smoke?'

'You're wanted by Mr Burgess.'

Eli laid his pipe aside, grumbling loudly, and made his
way onto the quarterdeck where Dónal later saw him deep
in conversation with the first mate. But everyone's
attention was directed at the ship that was slowly gaining

on them. Mr Munro had told Joe Quane that with his telescope he had seen a bow-chaser run out, and unless they could keep well ahead of her until nightfall, this could give them trouble. A bow-chaser was a gun that fired directly forwards. In a chase like this, in which one of the ships was trying hard to outrun the other, a lucky shot from the bow-chaser could hole a sail and slow down the boat, or even bring down a mast. Even slight damage could make it easier for the chasing ship to catch up.

The captain came on deck now, looking woebegone and very little aware of what was happening. Mr Burgess explained the situation to him in a kindly, patient voice and he nodded his understanding. Dónal heard him say, 'You have everything well in hand, Davey. I'll just go below and get a little shut-eye before the shooting starts.'

Just before dark, Mr Burgess ordered a dim light lit on the stern, one that might look a little like the light of a steering compass. Everyone wondered at this, since the light would make it easier for the pirate ship to follow them. Joe Quane was heard to declare that 'Burgess was in league with the pirates'. But the captain came on deck briefly at seven bells in the first watch, saw the light and said nothing. He looked better now and his 'shut-eye' seemed to have done him some good. The chase-ship showed no lights, of course, and since there was no moon she could not be made out.

Eli Twiss came on deck again at the change of watch and he and Burgess conferred for a time. Then, very quietly, Burgess ordered a ship's boat put over the side. 'And not a sound, mind, not a squeak from a tackle.' The men obeyed and the boat was lowered silently onto the sea. Now Eli Twiss reappeared carrying a short stubby mast. He handed it to Dónal and climbed over the side into the boat. Then the mast was handed down.

In the darkness Dónal could not see what Eli was doing, but when he began to hammer loudly, cursing as he worked, Dónal was horrified. This sound and the light would tell the pirate ship exactly where they were. He wanted to protest to Mr Burgess, but stopped himself, remembering that the mate could have no good reason for betraying them to Barbary pirates. In time the hammering stopped.

'All shipshape,' came the voice of Eli.

'Right then. Stand by.' Mr Burgess walked back to the quarterdeck and hissed a command to the helmsman. Then he disappeared down the companionway to emerge a moment later carrying a shaded lantern. He brought it along the deck, careful all the time to keep its light low, and handed it over the side to Eli Twiss. Now by the dim light Dónal could see that Eli had fixed the makeshift mast in the stern of the boat and he was now attaching the lantern to it. In the darkness he had also set up the boat's own little mast and had a small sail ready to be raised.

'Ready,' he hissed.

Mr Burgess turned to the quarterdeck. 'Now!'

Dónal saw the dim light on the quarterdeck go out and at the same time, the shade was taken off the lantern in the boat.

'Make sail, Twiss,' Mr Burgess hissed, and immediately Eli raised the boat's sail. In a flash he had set it and leaped back onto the *Provident*, hauling himself up by a rope and surprising Dónal with his agility. Mr Burgess slipped the lines that held the boat in place and they watched it drift away from the *Provident*'s side. Soon the wind caught the little square sail and the boat scudded along in their wake like one of the pleasure-craft that Dónal had seen at home in Cork Harbour.

'Now, all hands,' said Mr Burgess. 'Stand by the sheets and braces. We'll alter course.'

He walked back to the helm and very slowly the ship began to change course, the helmsman making very slow alterations on the wheel. As she turned to sail a more northerly course, and across the winds at a sharper angle, she began to heel more.

Dónal watched the little boat with her bobbing light continue on her merry way, following the same course that the *Provident* had been following a few minutes before, and he realised that this was a trick devised by Mr Burgess. They had shown a light since nightfall and, no doubt, the pirate captain was delighted to see it, thinking that they had made a mistake and not covered the compass light. He had been following it for hours now and, Dónal hoped, would continue to follow the light for the rest of the night. With luck the *Provident* would be out of sight by daybreak and the pirates would be gone.

Dónal's thoughts were disturbed by an elbow in the ribs. 'He's a cute one, Burgess?' It was his uncle. 'Don't be mistaken, Dónal *a stór*,' he said, breathing brandy fumes on Dónal. 'Burgess is a man on his way down. Clap onto Mr Munro and you'll rise with him.'

'Michael Long, you are little better than a turncoat. Get away from me.'

'You'll thank your old uncle yet, my lad. You'll see.'

The crew turned in at eight bells, gleefully happy with Mr Burgess's trick. Eli Twiss, in particular, returned to his pipe with great satisfaction. 'That be the end of them, Dónal,' he said between puffs. 'Now turn in.'

When dawn came it was clear that the trick had not worked. The ship was still there when Dónal came on deck, though slightly further off. The officers were all on deck studying her through their telescopes.

Flying from her mainmast was a huge British flag. Dónal rubbed his eyes in disbelief. She was a British ship after all, not the dreaded Barbary pirates!

They would heave to now, and an officer would come aboard as had happened earlier. Dónal and Mr Burgess would reveal the rows of chained slaves to him and all would be well. He would be serving on board a man-of-war again in a matter of hours. He could almost dance with joy.

He went in search of Eli Twiss at once and found him again filling wooden buckets with nails and bits of timber.

'What are you doing, Eli?'

'Case-shot,' Eli replied, gesturing at the buckets.

Dónal laughed with delight. The ship's carpenter still thought there was to be a fight!

'Eli! Haven't you heard the news? She's a British sloop. Look out and you'll see the ensign!'

Eli sat down and directed a look of pity at Dónal. 'Reckon it's a trick, boy. You'll see what colours she wears when she comes in range. And they'll be black.'

Dónal would not believe it.

''Tis true. It's no more'n a low pirate trick.'

Sure enough within the hour the red ensign was hauled down and a huge black flag run up in its place. Dónal remembered the words of a song he used to hear sung on the *Leander*. 'And there neath her rigging black colours she wore.' In that song the pirate ship had been defeated and sunk and Dónal wondered whether this time it would be the *Provident* that fell silent and vanished beneath the waves.

Now the pirate came on quickly, as though the flag itself had lent her speed. Hardly had it begun to fly than there was a puff of smoke at her bow and a spout of water away to leeward of them. The bow-chaser was firing.

The deck of the *Provident* burst into frantic activity as the gun crews attempted to turn the guns so as to fire as much backwards as possible. Mr Munro and Mr Burgess stalked between them, encouraging and shouting directions. Captain Pearson stood on the quarterdeck anxiously staring astern.

The second shot from the bow-chaser was closer, the third closer still, so close in fact that its spout of water threw spray onto the deck. Mr Burgess muttered that they were getting the range and Mr Munro ordered his gun crews to pray for deliverance.

'Mr Burgess, I intend to turn to starboard. Be so good as to have your guns ready to fire in time.' Captain Pearson sounded more like his old self, calm and in command. Dónal felt a surge of hope – perhaps they would put up a fight after all.

The fourth shot from the bow-chaser whistled through the rigging over Dónal's head, missing everything by some miracle.

'That was a good shot, Cap'n,' Mr Burgess shouted. 'They have someone who can lay a gun.'

'Three and a half minutes, I reckon,' the captain said. 'It takes 'em three and a half minutes to load and fire that bow-chaser. Stand by. I'll turn just before they fire if I can.' Dónal could see what he was doing. If he could turn just before the bow-chaser got off another shot they would surely miss, and the *Provident*'s guns might have a chance of doing some damage to them.

'Bring her round!' The order was delivered in a steady voice and the helmsman spun the wheel immediately. The ship's head swung off the wind, the angle of the decks increased dramatically while hands desperately eased the sheets, and the enemy fired again. Dónal saw the ball land in the water far ahead and to larboard just before their own guns started firing. Three guns went off, one after the other, the fourth being kept for close work and loaded with case-shot still. Then the ship began to swing back on course.

Dónal saw all three balls fall far short of their target and heard Mr Burgess giving the orders to sponge and clean the barrels. None of the gun crews really knew how to fight their piece, he noticed. They squabbled over whose job it was to sponge, and wasted time getting in each other's way. At length they had the guns run out again and immediately the ship began to swing.

'Fire as she bears, Mr Burgess,' said Captain Pearson.

Again the pirate gun fired, followed immediately by their own first and second guns. Gun number three failed to fire on time because the slow match with which the powder was fired had simply gone out. Again there was no damage to the pirate ship, though the she was now no more than a quarter of a mile away.

Before they could swing again the pirate's bow-chaser got its next shot off. Dónal heard the shot crash into the rigging and felt the impact in the timbers he was standing on. Immediately Eli Twiss and others were swarming upwards. Dónal saw them swinging up into the topmast shrouds with spare rope slung round their shoulders. But they could not save the topmast. With the ropes that held it shot away on one side, it leant forward under the pressure of the sail. Even from deck Dónal could see the strain on the timbers. Then with a loud tearing sound it broke and pitched forward carrying sails and rigging with it. The crew looked up dumbfounded.

Across the water they could hear cheering on the pirate ship. There were people dancing up and down and waving their arms on deck.

Captain Pearson stepped forward to the taffrail and bellowed at the crew to man their guns. Dónal heard Mr Burgess telling his men that they would have to fight now, fight for their lives. On the other side Mr Munro was swinging the guns straight again.

'Right, lads,' Captain Pearson shouted. 'One more shot on my orders, then quick as you can, everyone loads with case-shot. Then cutlasses all hands and every man for himself. May God have mercy on us all.'

Now Dónal became aware of the wailing of the slaves between the decks. Any shot that pierced the hull of the ship would go through their deck, where there was not an inch of clearance, and if the ship sank there would be no saving the slaves. Dónal did not think that the seamen would even give them a thought.

Captain Pearson brought the ship round again, sailing broadside on to the pirate. Everyone watched for the signal as the pirate ship came steadily down on them, closing, closing. They could see the faces staring steadily at them, dark faces and bright eyes, colourful clothes, curved swords and boarding pikes at the ready.

'Fire!'

This time four guns went off and four guns struck home at the close range. Two shots went high and tore into the sails. One was accurate enough to sweep away ten feet of bulwark, but the fourth gun, loaded with case-shot, came as a surprise to the pirates. Dónal counted seven or eight men hit. He could hear their screams and imagined the rusty nails and scraps of iron piercing their skin. They would die a slow and painful death, or survive maimed for life.

The broadside had a strange effect on the pirate ship. Instead of closing the last few hundred yards she veered away and came broadside on to the *Provident*. Now the two ships were sailing almost parallel and Captain Pearson ordered the guns reloaded.

'She means to kill as many of us as possible before she boards us. To make an easy fight of it.'

The pirate's gun deck began firing almost at once, eight guns against the *Provident*'s four. The range was close and several of the guns were manned by men who knew what they were doing. The balls came crashing down on the *Provident*, tearing shrouds and stays, smashing timber and men and guns. People fell where they stood and bled quietly along the decks, or rolled around clutching their wounds. Overhead the balls tore at the rigging and splintered the masts and spars. A yard came down on the fore hatch and went straight through. The deck shuddered underfoot from the impact of shot.

The *Provident* could not keep pace. Her ragged firing missed most of the time. The case-shot was not so effective after the first discharge because the pirate crew kept low and presented less of a target.

The men looked desperately to Captain Pearson for orders but no orders came from him. He stood helplessly on the quarterdeck, staring at the enemy. Sometimes he wiped his sleeve across his eyes as though wiping away tears, but Dónal could see that there were no tears.

'What will we do, Mr Burgess?' Dónal realised that the first mate was the only man who could help now.

Mr Burgess glanced at the captain and then at the pirate ship. He whirled round and shouted for Munro to take over command of his guns. 'Dónal, get Gideon Blood's gun, and his powder and shot. Look lively, there's no time to lose.'

When Dónal came back on deck, his arms weighed down by the huge musket, Gideon Blood was chewing tobacco on the quarterdeck, as calm and unruffled as he had been on the seashore in Benin. He took the gun from Dónal's hands and patted the stock.

'Gideon,' said Mr Burgess, 'you see that there pirate on the quarterdeck. The fellow with one eye. Could you hit him?'

'Reckon so.'

'Hit him then. A silver dollar if you hit him. I think he's their chief.'

Gideon Blood spat a stream of brown tobacco juice at the deck. 'Don't need no silver dollar to save my neck.'

He loaded the gun with care and knelt to rest it on the rail. 'Stand off there,' he told them. 'Had to put in more powder'n usual. She might blow up.'

Dónal stepped back quickly, suddenly reminded of a man he had met in prison in Waterford who had been blinded by a backfiring musket.

This time there was even more smoke and flame than usual, almost as much as from one of the cannons. Dónal saw the man on the pirate ship punched backwards by the force of the shot. He fell against the rail of his own ship and was immediately hidden by a group of his men. By the time Gideon had reloaded they had carried the man below. Now Mr Burgess pointed out one of the gunners.

'He's their best gunner. Every ball from that gun strikes home. Hit him and there's another silver . . . !'

Bang! The gunner somersaulted backwards and the stunned gun crew looked desperately around for their leader.

'Mighty good shooting, Gideon! Man, that was the best shot I ever saw!'

For the first time in days Dónal saw Gideon smile.

'Now, look there. That's a powder keg. Or else it's water. Shoot that and we'll find out.'

Dónal saw that the gun crew at the forward gun had foolishly brought a powder keg to their gun. It was in full view and would present an easier target than a man.

Gideon stared down the barrel of his gun for a full minute before he pulled the trigger and this time the explosion of the gun was dwarfed by the blast on the enemy ship. A whoosh of flame enveloped the foredeck and the forward gun disappeared into it. Immediately there were five or six secondary explosions, smaller powder charges already prepared for the gun. Two men fell out into the sea and a third ran along the deck with his clothes and hair on fire. He was knocked unceremoniously into the sea by one of his mates before he could set off any more powder.

During all this Gideon was steadily reloading his gun. 'What next, Mr Burgess?'

'The man with the hat.'

Dónal had seen this man stalking up and down behind the guns and had concluded that he was a pirate officer, as important perhaps as the first man that Gideon had hit.

Again Gideon fired. The shot struck the man full in the chest and it was plain to Dónal that it had killed him. This had a dramatic effect on the pirate ship. Several of the gun crews left their guns and ran to the body. The helmsman put down the helm at the same time, without any visible sign of an order, causing the ship to bear away from the *Provident*. The guns that were still manned fired, but because of the changed course their shots went wide and fell in the sea.

But most important of all, Dónal could see that the fire on the forward part of the ship where Gideon had hit the powder barrel had taken hold of some of the timbers and spread into the sails. Smoke clouded the whole front of the ship and frantic efforts were being made to put the flames out. After months, maybe years, of sailing under a hot sun, the pirate ship would be as dry as tinder, Dónal knew. The fire would keep them occupied a long time.

At the same time their own four guns went off and two balls struck, one piercing the pirate ship just above the water line, the second ripping into a boat that was lashed down between the masts. Dónal could easily imagine the damage done by splinters from that boat. He had seen it before. Suddenly he was heartsick of battle and made up his mind that if he did survive the voyage he would not return to the navy, but live out his days as a fisherman or merchant sailor in some peaceful trade far from pirates and slavers.

7
___

MUTINY

All through that night they watched the ghostly fire take hold of the pirate ship. The two ships had separated, but the *Provident* was so badly damaged that Mr Burgess dared not make sail to escape. Instead Eli Twiss and the able hands worked at the masts and yards to make them safe. Below decks teams of men patched sails and rove new shrouds and stays. Still others carried the dead on deck and tipped them over the side. Fifteen men lay wounded or dying on the quarterdeck. When the yard had gone through the hatch it had killed two slaves. A ball had gone straight through the slave deck killing seven and wounding as many more. Another had carried away the support of the upper slave deck where it met the forward bulkhead of the hold, and the upper deck had collapsed onto the lower. Twenty Africans suffocated there while the battle was raging on deck. Mr Munro dropped their bodies over the side, together, Dónal was sure, with uncounted sick and wounded.

Dónal had seen more care for human life on the deck

of a man-of-war, a ship dedicated to killing. Here on the deck of a slaver, human life, white or black, was less valuable than the ship's timbers or the owner's profit. What he was witnessing, he realised, was evil taking hold of the hearts of men. It was a frightening sight and he knew that unless he could escape it the pollution would spread to his own soul and eat it up, as it had eaten the souls of Mr Munro and Captain Pearson.

Then as darkness fell, the flames became clear, a dim flickering along the horizon's edge, a kind of floating picture of hell. He knew it was the pirate ship and, although he knew the terror of fire at sea, a kind of relief flooded in because the flames meant the pirates would be too busy to think about attacking them again. By the time the fire was out the *Provident* might well be fit to make full sail. Perhaps they had a chance to outrun their enemy now.

Captain Pearson had locked himself into his cabin shortly after the battle and there was no call for Dónal's service. Mister Burgess supervised the repairs while Mr Munro tended to the wounded. Dónal noticed that his uncle was as busy as anyone, serving up hot soup to his favourites, helping to throw the dead overboard, following Mr Munro around like a lapdog. More and more Dónal regretted that he had ever rescued the man. But for his help, Michael Long could be rotting in the penal colony in New South Wales by now.

All night the flames flickered on the horizon and, as time went by, Dónal could see that those flames were growing brighter and stronger. It seemed to him that the flames symbolised the evil power that was at work on that warm and welcoming sea. By the middle watch he climbed up to the foretop where he could occasionally see the outline of masts and spars in the flame. Eli Twiss was there, splicing rigging that had been cut through.

He jerked a thumb towards the fire. 'The gates o' hell, Dónal.'

Dónal was struck by the fact that Eli's mind had been running on the same thoughts as his. 'And what about us, Eli? Slavers, that's what we are. Are we any better? How much difference is there between a pirate and a slaver?'

Eli's cackling laugh shocked Dónal. 'Why, we got the law on our side, boy! You cain't go to hell if you got the law on your side!'

The other sailors watched the fire too. Sometimes they looked up from their work and stared grimly at the distant glow. None of them took any satisfaction from the sight, with their superstitious dread of fire at sea.

Mr Burgess found Dónal and enquired about Captain Pearson.

'He's below, sir. Locked in his cabin. I can't raise a sound from him though I've knocked often and often, and called.'

'It'll be the pipe, Dónal. He'll be smoking and sleeping. Did you see him during the battle?'

Dónal nodded.

'I'll seize the ship tomorrow,' continued Mr Burgess. 'I spoke Gideon Blood and he'll stand with us. He's sick of the trade too.'

Dónal's heart leaped.

'At eight bells in the morning watch I'll take an axe to the captain's cabin door. You and Gideon Blood will witness what we find there and I'll enter you both as witnesses in the log.'

'I'll do it,' Dónal said.

The mate's eyes wandered to the horizon. 'I can't say as I pity them,' he said. 'But I wouldn't wish for it. Fire at sea is a terrible thing.'

At eight bells Gideon Blood took up an axe on Mr Burgess's order and smashed the lock on the captain's door. They found Captain Pearson lying on his bunk with his hands folded across his chest, a cloth over his eyes. On the floor beside him lay the strange pipe.

'Captain Pearson, I have to inform you that I no longer consider you competent to manage the ship. I hereby take command.'

Mr Burgess stood by the captain's bedside as he spoke but the captain made no response. Dónal stepped forward with rising horror and removed the cloth from the captain's eyes. He expected to find that the captain was dead. What he saw shocked him more deeply. Captain Pearson's eyes were enormously swollen and red, and yellow pus encrusted them, sealing them shut. There was a new smell in the cabin, like the smell of a dead animal. Dónal stepped back, dropping the cloth as he did so.

Suddenly the captain's firm voice issued from the ruined face. 'Now you know my little secret, Davey Burgess. I thought to hide it a few days more. But you see it now.'

'In the name of God what is it?' The first mate was suddenly less certain of himself.

'Trachoma, I believe the surgeons call it. I'm blind, Davey. Or as near blind as makes no difference.'

'How long?'

'I don't know. It's been coming on a while. I've been smoking my pipe, Davey, since we left Africa. I've lost my course a bit. I haven't been keeping the log even.'

'How did it happen?'

'Oh, it happens easy enough. It's the trade, you see. The flesh. They bring it aboard with them from their cursed swamps. It spreads like wildfire. You have to get rid of it fast. That's what Munro is doing, getting rid of the blind ones. You can't sell a blind blackbird. But the blackbirds can sing now, Davey. They have their revenge. You may take out that wicked knife of yours and cut my throat this minute and I will thank you for it.' His face cracked into a smile. 'You have to take the ship now. And if you don't take her to Jamaica they'll cut your throat, the men. The ship is yours. And the flesh. And may God have mercy on your soul.'

Mr Burgess shook his head grimly. 'I wasn't born a fool, Nathaniel Pearson. I'm not the only man you brought aboard under false pretences. There's plenty of seamen here that thought they were on a trading voyage. Plenty of them have no taste for slaving.'

'Aye. But you see, Davey, they have the jingle of the money in their ears. Blackbirds make fortunes and I offered them a piece of the fortune. It's in the articles they signed for. How many of them will stand by you now?' Again the cracked lips twisted into a smile.

The mate beckoned to Gideon and Dónal to follow him out. 'Gideon, take your musket up onto the quarterdeck as quietly as you can. Don't let anyone else up there. Shoot if you must. Dónal, here is the key to the small arms locker. Bring everything you can to my cabin, especially the pistols. Come up to the quarterdeck when you are ready.'

Dónal worked feverishly to carry the pistols and muskets to the mate's cabin. There was a pistol for almost every man on board because the captain had been prepared for trouble. There were fewer muskets but these were heavier. He was carrying a load past the steps that led to the deck when a shadow fell in front of him. Before he had time to step back he had been seen. Joe Quane was standing on the top step, a puzzled look on his face. The puzzlement delayed Quane's reaction long enough for Dónal to sidestep quickly into the mate's room, slam the door and bolt it. He heard Quane roar and leap from the step. He heard his shoulder slam into the cabin door and saw that the bolt would soon splinter and break out of its receiver.

As quickly as he could, Dónal loaded a pistol as Gideon Blood had shown him, while Quane launched himself against the door a second and third time.

Now the gun was loaded and cocked and Dónal stepped back so as to be behind the door when it burst open, while at the same time being as far away from it as possible. He watched the bolt bulge and the wood splinter. Would he be able to hit Quane? He remembered the way the gun jumped in his hand. He remembered Gideon's advice to aim low and lowered the barrel. But would the shot stop Quane? It was still possible that Quane would knife him, bullet wound or no bullet wound.

But before he had to put his shooting to the test he heard Mr Burgess's voice. 'I would shoot you without the slightest doubt, Joe Quane.'

Joe Quane's bluster: 'He's stealin' the guns!'

'Get forward where you belong, Quane,' and the scuttle of Joe Quane's feet. Then a tap at the door. 'Dónal, he's gone. Bring six pistols and powder and shot. Lock the door when you leave. The key is on my table.'

Dónal slid back the bolt, uncocked the pistol, gathered as many as his arms could carry, picked up the key and backed out through the door. He closed the door carefully and turned the key in the lock.

Up on deck the crew were gathering, some curious, some angry, some indifferent. They stood in a loose knot, facing aft to the quarterdeck. When Dónal emerged onto that deck with the load of pistols in his arms there was a murmur among them and Dónal's uncle stepped forward.

'Come with us, Dónal boy. Don't turn on your mates.'

'Is that the way it is, Michael Long?' Dónal turned his back on his uncle and walked to the far side of the deck.

Mr Burgess had set up a small swivel cannon on a special mounting on the quarterdeck and it was pointed straight at the crew. Gideon Blood leant on his musket in his usual loose-limbed way, chewing the eternal lump of tobacco. Dónal recognised the helmsman as Willie Austin, a seaman he had often heard expressing his dislike of slavery.

As he passed out the pistols he caught sight of Mr Munro emerging through the hatch in the slave deck grating.

'Now hear this, all hands,' said Burgess. 'Cap'n Pearson being ill, he has passed the command of the ship to me. As of eight bells in this morning's watch I am the cap'n.'

'Seizing the ship!' The shout could have been from any one of the crew.

'By order of Cap'n Pearson, I said.' Mr Burgess scarcely raised his voice.

'That so? Why'ja need the guns?'

This comment drew a murmur of agreement from the crowd. Others shouted now. 'Mutiny!' 'You'll swing!'

'Silence on deck!' His authority was still there. 'I will lay it on the line for you, boys. This is the truth of it. I intend to turn her round and beat back to Africa. I'm going to put the slaves ashore there just as soon as I can, and I'm a-going to pick up a cargo of timber and ivory. The ivory'll sell as well as slaves in Jamaica.'

'What you goin' to buy her with?' Joe Quane's was the voice this time, clear as a bell.

'You leave that to me, Joe Quane. You mind your business.'

Now there was angry talk among the men.

Joe Quane spoke again. 'We'll see thee in hell first, before we turn back. I'm with Mr Munro. We'll sell the slaves in Jamaica and divide the money between us.' The group of men around Joe Quane was edging towards the steps that led to the quarterdeck and Mr Burgess had the match for the little cannon in his hand.

'Joe, let me explain something to you. First, this here swivel gun is loaded with case-shot. I reckon I could flatten you and your mates with one shot. Next, the cap'n is sick. What he is sick with is the white blindness.' Shock among the men. 'That's right. He'll be stone blind in a week or so. And he won't be the last. The slaves brought it on board. It's a judgement of God on all of us. If we

don't bring them back to where they came from every man
on this ship will go blind. Remember the *Leon*.'

Now they were panicked. Burgess had them in the palm
of his hand.

'Turn 'er round!' someone shouted.

'God help us!'

'Witchcraft!'

Mr Munro stepped forward and raised his hands for
silence. 'I've just come from the slave decks. There are
four cases of blindness there too. And one or two fevers.
If this is God's judgement then he must be punishing the
blackbirds too. I say we run on to Jamaica. It will take us
as long to beat back against the trade winds as it will to
run on with the trades abaft the beam.'

Mr Burgess surveyed the crew from the lofty height of
the quarterdeck. 'It's as simple as this, boys. You can side
with me, the lawful master of this ship and the man in
possession of the quarterdeck and the swivel gun. Or you
can side with Mr Munro, who if he utters one more word
against me becomes a mutineer on the spot and will be
so recorded in the ship's log. So step forward now if you
want to be on the side of righteousness.'

A movement in the crowd revealed Eli Twiss, his
carpenter's tool-bag still slung across his shoulder, having
spent all night working.

'I'm with you, Mr Burgess.' But before he could put a
step on the ladder to climb up to them Joe Quane's knife
flashed out and Eli fell to the ground holding his side. In
the stunned silence Joe Quane looked to Mr Munro, a
foolish grin on his face. Munro looked on, unmoved.

Then Mr Burgess stepped forward, a pistol in his hand.

'Joe Quane, I arrest you for stabbing a shipmate.'

Quane looked around for help and found only stony faces. He looked down at his knife, the blade red with the carpenter's blood, then up at the steady barrel of the pistol pointed at his chest.

'Drop the knife and step up here.'

Quane dropped the knife and walked quietly onto the quarterdeck.

'Dónal and Gideon, go down and get Eli. Look lively.'

Eli Twiss was not dead. When Dónal bent to take him under the arm the old ship's carpenter winked up at him and whispered, 'Easy, boy. I'm leakin' at the seams!'

They carried him up and laid him in the shade. Gideon tore his shirt and stuffed the wound. 'Reckon you'll live,' was all he said.

Three other men had come over to the first mate's side and they were now standing at the taffrail, armed with pistols.

'Now, men,' Mr Burgess said. 'Stand by to wear ship.' There was no movement among the crew.

Mr Munro threw a triumphant look at the quarterdeck. 'You cannot work a ship without us, Burgess. Now, lads, in the name of God get up to the fo'c'sle.' There was a slight hesitation before the men turned and ran. Although Mr Burgess levelled the swivel gun again, he could not bring himself to fire on them and they made their way safely to the shelter of the fo'c'sle.

'We're in a pretty way now,' Mr Burgess said. 'Seven men to work the ship all the way back to Africa. It cannot be done.'

But Gideon Blood was staring out at the sea. 'Boat, sir.

Over yonder.' They followed his outstretched hand and saw a boat with a tattered sail set. The *Provident* had still not got under way after the repairs of the night, though she could now set sail if there was a crew to do it. So the little boat came towards them at quite a pace. Before long they could see that it was a ship's lifeboat with one man at the helm and several others in various attitudes of exhaustion aboard. The sail was run full out and as the boat yawed from side to side in the waves the sail was taken aback from time to time and the little boom that held it swept across the boat and crashed over on the other side.

'The man must be wore down,' said Willie Austin. 'He cain't even steer no more.'

As the boat closed with the *Provident* it became clear to Dónal that she was a lifeboat, and something about the man at the helm told him that this was part of the pirate crew.

The boat passed within thirty yards of the *Provident* without altering course and continued on ahead. Dónal realised with a shock that the men on the boat were all dead. As they passed he could see that the helmsman was horribly burned, his face bared to the bone. The others on board were little more than charred flesh

8

RATS IN A BARREL

They made their preparations as best they could. First, Mr Burgess went below and brought up clean cloth to dress Eli's wound. He bound it up tight, then propped the old ship's carpenter on a sail, facing forward. The old man joked constantly about his wound. He told them all how he had been struck by an arrow while his ship lay at anchor in Tierra Del Fuego, riding out a hurricane; how the arrowhead had been buried so deep that the surgeon had decided it was easier to push it through than cut it out.

'That's enough of your tales, Eli Twiss. I reckon you have more stories than a storybook writer.' Mr Burgess was smiling as he spoke.

'Every word is God's truth,' protested Eli. 'Ain't a word of a lie.'

Gideon was given the job of loading and priming all the pistols. Each man was issued with two guns and a cutlass and one of the sailors who had come over to them was placed on guard in the first mate's cabin and told to load and prime every musket. Joe Quane was bound hand and foot and tied to the stern rail. Then all hands were issued with water rations.

'Reckon they won't come out for a bit. Dónal, go below and speak the captain. See how he gets along.'

Dónal dreaded that task. He knocked at the broken door and was told to 'Step in'.

'I came to enquire after you, sir.' Dónal's voice was unsteady.

'Sure you did, boy. Step up to me here. How do I look now?'

'Well enough, sir.'

'Don't tell lies, boy. How do my eyes look?'

Dónal looked at the swollen, encrusted lumps that were his eyelids. 'Bad enough, sir.'

'That's the truth all right. It'll settle down in time. Do you know what then? Well, boy, I'll be sand-blind, dark as midnight. You can't be a blind sea-captain.'

Dónal was filled with pity. 'Poor Captain Pearson.'

'Aye, well may you say "Poor Captain Pearson". Tell me, what has that bilge-rat Davey Burgess done with my ship? Why aren't we under way?'

Dónal explained what had happened.

'I knew it. He's dead set against slaving, you see. He did it once before and he got conscience. The man has no stomach. Conscience is a mighty bad thing at sea; never a voyage but you have to do something against conscience. All's hard work and danger out here on the deep, boy. Maybe you lose a hand overboard and you can't turn the brig around in case she oversets in a heavy sea. That's a man lost to your conscience. Maybe you have to flog a man because he wouldn't obey his officer and you know the officer's the wrong one. That's a man flogged against your conscience. Go to sea with whatever you like, Dónal, but leave your conscience ashore. What's a black man to Davey Burgess? Does he eat of his bread? Sup with him? What's one black man more or less? Or a hundred? Or five hundred? But no, Davey Burgess must be worried about him.'

He paused. 'A drink of water, Dónal?' Dónal lifted a cup to his parched mouth. 'I had to trick him, you see. He would never have come on this voyage otherwise. And Davey Burgess, damned abolitionist that he is, is the best seaman I ever sailed with.'

He was silent for a moment.

'What would those fellows in your old country say to me? The ones the British hanged a year ago?'

'The United Irishmen?'

'The rebels, the very ones.'

Dónal considered a moment.

'Mostly they hate slavery. They wouldn't like you, Captain Pearson, that's the truth of it. Nor they don't like chains and flogging. I shudder to think what my poor father would say to me if he was alive, to see his own son on a slaving ship!'

While he was speaking, Dónal had soaked a towel and now he began to mop at the captain's face. At first he protested and waved Dónal away, but after a while he lay still.

'You're a kindly boy, Dónal Long. I rue the day I shipped you.'

'Why is that, sir? I have done my duty as best I could.'

'Not for that, not for that. No, boy. I'm sorry to have brought you on an ill-starred ship. Looky here, it's true what that old pilot said. There's no luck in a slaving ship. It's all greed and no humanity.

'Look at me now,' he continued. 'I put myself on the side of the Lord of Darkness, treating these poor black-amoors like animals. No man should do that to his fellow man, Dónal. I confess it. I have done mostly harm in my life, and very little good. And I have been punished with darkness.'

Dónal sponged the suppurating wounds that once were the captain's eyes, and he reflected that Captain Pearson had indeed been visited with darkness, darkness of the eye and darkness of the mind.

On deck all was quiet.

Eli Twiss slept while Willie Austin and Mr Burgess kept watch. Joe Quane stared malevolently about him. The tropical sun shone down on the idle deck with blistering intensity. Melted tar dripped from the masts and yards. Dónal could almost feel the timbers drying and shrinking under his feet. There was no shade on the quarterdeck and there was precious little water anywhere on board. He wondered what his uncle was thinking, up there in the stifling oven of the fo'c'sle. And he wondered how a man who had fought for the liberty of Irishmen in the 1798 rebellion could now throw in his lot with people who wanted to enslave other human beings because their skin colour was different. Dónal was certain that had his father been still alive he would be with him now, fighting alongside Mr Burgess and Gideon Blood and Willie Austin and Eli Twiss and the others. The memory returned to him of his uncle beating him with the buckle of his belt in their cottage in Ballymonas so many thousands of miles away across the ocean. And the old hatred came back. What was the man only a whinging coward who would always take what he thought was the winning side? But he was wrong-shipped this time anyway. The mutineers would not win against Mr Burgess. After all, even Captain Pearson admitted that Burgess was the best seaman he had ever sailed with.

'They must come along the deck, Dónal,' Mr Burgess said. 'In full view. They can't come through the hold because when we put in the slave decks we closed off the hatches. What they should do is wait us out. Once night falls they can creep up on us. But they won't do that. That fo'c'sle is like an oven now, with the sun frying them all. Their tempers'll rise and Munro is not man enough to manage them. He'll say a few prayers and charge us as quick as the rest of them. They'll come down the deck screaming blue murder and when they get to the steps yonder, why we'll open fire, and any that get past the shot will meet with our swords as they come over the rail. Fear naught, Dónal boy. We'll carry the day for sure.'

'I'm rightly ashamed of my uncle, Mr Burgess. He was a United Irishman in the recent rebellion and I expected that if he could fight for the liberty of his fellow countrymen, he would defend the liberty of the Africans as well.'

'Never as easy as that, Dónal. And think you, there are problems yet. Consider what we will do with those same Africans. I'm afeard if we bring them on deck they will turn on us. And yet how can we keep them chained below decks? It is intolerable.'

'We could maybe let them out some at a time. And ease their suffering by giving them more space. We could keep some of them on deck by night.'

Mr Burgess looked brightly at Dónal. 'You're right, boy. We can do that. It will do nicely, and it will help with their health too. We have to try to make them understand us.'

They were interrupted by the sound of voices raised in anger in the fo'c'sle and immediately Willie Austin woke the others. They stood to their guns for a time, listening carefully, but they could not make out a single clear word.

Then the door on the starboard side opened and a white handkerchief tied to the end of a capstan bar came into view. It was followed by the head of the bosun, whose name was Rice. 'Parley,' he called. 'We wants to parley.'

'Is Munro afraid to come out himself?'

'No sir, but I'm to do the parley anyways.'

The bosun advanced nervously to the middle of the deck. Eli Twiss laughed scornfully at him. 'Bosun Rice the deeplomat! Tommy Rice, you ain't got enough sense to heave up yer anchor when the storm's a-comin'.'

The bosun tried to maintain his dignity by ignoring the carpenter. 'I'm to offer ya terms, sir.'

Mr Burgess snorted. 'Terms? What terms?'

'If'n ya surrender, we'll give ya a boat'n stores, water'n a sail. Take who ya want. We'll go our way and you go yourn.'

'And if our boat reaches the West Indies a month, six months or a year after you, and some of us are alive, what then?'

Dónal could see the bosun struggling to follow the

implications of what the mate was saying.

Rice smiled broadly. 'Why, good luck to ya.'

'Aye,' said Mr Burgess, 'and will you wish us good luck when we have you hunted down for mutiny? Will you bid us good day when you step onto the gallows?'

The bosun's face clouded again. 'Ya wouldn't do that now, sir? Not after we treated you fair and square?'

'I would hunt you down myself, you rat. Hanging is too good for you. A slaver and a mutineer to boot!'

Eli Twiss's laugh again. 'Well said, Mr Mate! Hanging is too good for 'em!'

Another man stepped out of the fo'c'sle door. He waved a fist and came halfway along the deck to roar abuse at them. 'Come back here, Tommy Rice! Surrender or no, I'll see Burgess and that traitor Twiss fed to the sharks before this night is out!'

'Is that so, Thomas Benting, the murderer of helpless slaves?' Mr Burgess looked as though he were enjoying the shouting match. 'I know what you and Munro and Joe Quane have been doing. Killing off the weak. When we get to New England you'll swing for murder. A man is a man no matter what the colour of his skin and murder is still murder, even on the high seas.' He raised his voice so it would carry into the fo'c'sle more clearly. 'There's not one of you that is not tainted and polluted by this trade. I'll see you all dancing at the bitter end of a rope!'

At this Rice threw down his white flag and sprinted for cover.

'Look at him run!' Mr Burgess shouted. 'Cowards to a man!' Benting and Rice reached the fo'c'sle door at the same time and for a brief comical moment they were jammed shoulder to shoulder in the doorway. Then a hand reached up and hauled Rice through. Benting fell in after him and the door closed again.

In the middle of the afternoon, round about what would have been six bells if they had been ringing the bells, the crew rushed the quarterdeck. It was Eli Twiss who sounded the alarm. His bleeding had stopped and he was sitting comfortably enough. Mr Burgess still stood near the swivel gun but Gideon Blood had replaced Willie Austin as the second watch.

Eli Twiss was just about to ask for water when a movement caught his eye and he hissed for Mr Burgess. Everyone was alert at once, pistols cocked. Dónal laid his sword by the stern rail, cocked one pistol and loosened the other in his belt.

They came stealthily at first, slipping through the door, then dashing for the cover of the boats. Then with a shout Munro broke cover and ran, swinging a cutlass above his head. The other sailors followed, all screaming and waving their weapons. Dónal noticed that they had no guns, though all possessed cutlasses and knives. He also noticed that his uncle was not among the attackers.

'Steady now, boys,' Mr Burgess shouted. 'Wait for it.'

Dónal saw him pick up the slow match again. He saw him swivel the gun towards the steps. He saw him tip the match into the touch-hole and saw the gun go off. Then there were men on the rail, swinging over onto the quarterdeck, cutlasses raised.

Dónal fired straight into the chest of the man nearest him and saw his target fall off the rail. Then he switched hands and levelled the second pistol. Thomas Benting was in front of him, struggling to keep his grip on the rail with one hand and to swing his cutlass at Dónal with the second. Dónal fired. This time he missed. Now he ran back to the stern rail and picked up the cutlass he had left there. He turned quickly and saw Mr Burgess at swordpoint with Mr Munro. Benting was gone. Dónal ran at the second mate, cutlass low. The point struck Munro on his thigh and at the same time Mr Burgess struck the cutlass out of his hand. Munro fell backwards as the wounded leg folded under him. Out of the corner of his eye Dónal saw Eli Twiss firing a third pistol at someone on the main deck, then the noise stopped.

The attack was over, having lasted no more than a minute by Dónal's guess. Munro and three others lay wounded on the quarterdeck. Two more lay twisting in pain at the foot of the steps where the case-shot from the swivel gun had caught them. By the sound of the groaning coming from the fo'c'sle there were others wounded in there.

Eli Twiss was grinning contentedly and cleaning the barrel of his pistol. Two other pistols lay by his side. Gideon Blood had taken up his musket and was aiming it at the fo'c'sle door. Mr Burgess was dressing Munro's wound.

Gideon's gun went off and the ball crashed straight through the heavy wood of the door. Gideon grinned. 'Reckon I could shoot every one of 'em, right on through that old timber. Just like rats in a barrel.'

Mr Burgess told him to keep firing and Gideon grinned appreciatively.

'Everyone else, hear this. We've got to go after them.

Load up your pistols and stand by. Willie, tie up this mutineer here,' and Mr Burgess aimed a kick at Mr Munro's leg.

Willie Austin grinned. 'Truss him up like an ol' hog, I will!'

In ten minutes the prisoners were secured, Munro and Quane bound back to back, 'keepin' company' as Willie Austin said, and the pistols reloaded. In that time Gideon Blood had fired eight or nine shots and there were eight or nine holes at various levels in the fo'c'sle wall.

'Right. We didn't get Benting. And Tommy Rice ain't here either. We got to get them or they'll never give up. Come on. Follow me.'

Mr Burgess ran down the steps onto the main deck, followed by Gideon Blood, Willie Austin and Dónal. At the same time the fo'c'sle door opened and Rice, Benting and three or four more came out in a rush. The two sailors who had not followed now jumped the rail and charged with Mr Burgess.

The two parties met in the middle. Pistols were discharged first and two men fell dead. Then the swords clashed. Dónal found that the mutineers did not think him worth troubling over and so he was able to rush about lending a hand where necessary. The first to go down was Willie Austin, blood flowing from his stomach. Then a slave deck grating gave way and Thomas Benting fell through it.

Rice and Mr Burgess were fighting and both men had drawn blood. Without thinking, Dónal swung his cutlass and cut across the back of Rice's legs. The bosun sat backwards suddenly on his haunches, a surprised look on his face. Mr Burgess killed him where he sat, a sword-point through the heart.

With Rice and Benting gone, the fight petered out. The remaining mutineers emerged from the fo'c'sle looking glum, their hands in the air. Gideon Blood made them stand by the mainmast while Mr Burgess tried to stem the flow of blood from Willie Austin's wound. But there was little he could do. The boy died in his arms without a word.

9

A SINGLE SHOT

Mr Burgess surveyed the carnage. There was blood everywhere. The bulwarks were lined with the wounded – many of them bound to die before the night was out. There were not ten able-bodied men left in the boat. Given a week or two, enough men could be mustered to sail the ship, provided that none of the lesser wounds turned bad and gangrenous in the intolerable heat. But the *Provident* could not sit idle on the sea for a week, much less two. Food was rotting. The men were consuming water all the time. If the ship could not be got moving immediately they would all die of thirst before ever they reached land.

Rice was dead and his body had gone over the side before dark. A search found the body of Thomas Benting, who had fallen through the grating onto the slave deck. He had been strangled with chains. His body too went over the side. There were eight burials in all, Mr Burgess reading the service for them. When the burials were done and the remaining mutineers secured, the men lay down where they were and fell asleep in utter exhaustion.

Dónal searched the entire ship for his uncle but Michael Long was nowhere to be found.

'Murdered, do you think?' Mr Burgess only had half his mind on what Dónal was saying.

'He could be, aye,' Dónal replied. 'If anyone would take the trouble to do it. Bad luck to him anyway, for a mutineer. I don't care.' But he did care. A small part of his heart still told him that Michael Long was his uncle, and he regretted that his father's only brother had turned out to be such a sorry excuse for a man. But that was the end of it. There was too much to be done to think any further on it.

Once again Dónal was awakened by the slap of a flying fish, this time landing full on his face. He sat up and rubbed his eyes and listened. The creaking, heaving, groaning song of the ship was almost drowned out by the snoring of the sleepers and the groaning of the wounded. The tall figure of Mr Burgess still stood at the helm. Everywhere else there was chaos. The shrouds were tattered, the sails all partly unfurled, the yards crooked. There were dark patches on the deck where the blood had flowed, and brighter patches gleamed in the moonlight near the wounded.

Dónal's eyes filled with tears. A year before he had been a simple Irish boy whose greatest trouble was his drunken uncle. Now he had witnessed the evil in the heart of man and his life would never be the same again.

He struggled to his feet and made his way to the helm.

'What will we do, sir?' Mr Burgess said nothing. 'Will we make sail in the morning, sir, and beat back to Africa?'

'I was just wondering,' Mr Burgess spoke so quietly that Dónal had to lean forward to hear. 'I was just wondering whether that was a sail or no.' He pointed to the northeast, astern of them. Staring long at the gleaming sea, Dónal was just able to make out a shape that might have been the sails of a ship. 'If it is, it'll come up with us in the morning watch.'

'Will I call the men, sir? To ready the guns?'

'No point, boy.'

'But it might be pirates.'

'And what could we do? We could not fight two guns. We ain't about to sail this ship.'

'Turn us loose and we'll fight with you. We can settle our differences later.' It was Mr Munro, trussed up like an old hog as poor Willie Austin had said.

Mr Burgess smiled. 'If she wears the black flag, Mr Munro, you can rest assured that you won't fall into their hands alive.' Then he turned to Dónal. 'Go down and see how the cap'n is doing.'

The captain was awake and desperate. He sat up in his cot when he heard Dónal's step.

'For God's sake, Dónal boy. I must have my pipe. I can't find it. I've gone over this cabin twice and three times. Did you put it away, boy? With these eyes I can't see my way.'

'It's gone, Captain.'

The captain fell back on the pillows. 'Gone?'

'Orders from Mr Burgess. I threw it overboard!'

He had hardly uttered the words before the captain sprang from the bed and knocked him to the ground. 'I must have the opium!' he shouted. His hands grasped

Dónal's throat and Dónal felt his windpipe close. Desperately he flailed out with his fists, striking shoulders, head, face. He could not get air and he felt himself sinking into unconsciousness. He lost the strength of his arms.

Then he could breathe again. The air hurt his throat but his chest welcomed it and he was filled with a pleasurable sense of having escaped death. Gideon Blood was kneeling over him. Mr Burgess restrained the captain, pinning his arms to the bed as he raved and cursed.

'You were close to the wind there, boy,' Gideon Blood said. 'Near enough went west. I pulled him off.'

Dónal laughed at Gideon's way of understating everything. 'Oh Gideon, you saved my life.'

The captain raved and lashed out, demanding his opium. There were terrible things in his cabin, he told them, demons and sea monsters looking in the windows. He could not face them without opium. And the pain of his eyes was so bad. That was why he used the pipe.

'Settle down, Nathaniel.' Mr Burgess spoke soothingly. 'There's a ship bearing down on us. It'll all be over soon enough. Perhaps it's an American ship and she might have a surgeon. All will be well.' But in the end he and Gideon Blood had to rope the captain into his berth, his hands securely tied away from his face, his body bound to the bed.

'We'll have to watch him, boys. He's a wily old fox. He'll get out of those ropes and do some mischief if I know him.'

But by then all eyes were fixed on the white object astern of them, slowly growing into the shape of a ship under full sail in the moonlight. Every man who could stand was staring to windward. Even Eli Twiss had hauled himself into the rigging and was perched on the ratlines, his arms slung through the ropes to hold him in place.

'We gotta put up a fight,' Gideon Blood told them. 'We cain't just set here and wait for 'em to cut our throats. They's plenty of guns on board.' It was the strongest speech Dónal had ever heard from Gideon Blood.

Mr Burgess admitted the sense of what was being said. He counted the men who could do duty at a gun and decided they would load the two forward guns on each side. Whichever side the ship came down, the gun crews would fire the guns on that side. Mr Burgess was to captain one gun and Dónal was to captain the other.

'But, Mr Burgess, I have never even fired a gun.'

'Reckon you've seen more gunfiring than most of us. You tell them what to do and by God they'll do it. Gideon Blood, get up to the foretop with that musket of yours and kill anyone you can hit on the quarterdeck.'

'Stand by, men. She'll come up with us round about first light.'

A strange hope came over the men at the thought of this last desperate fight. They set to their tasks with a heart and a half, loading the guns and running them out, ready for action, joking as they worked. They particularly put their faith in Gideon's sharpshooting, remembering the explosion he had caused on the pirate ship, and consoling each other with the thought that any pirate might leave a keg or two of powder lying around on deck. As they worked, the moon went down and plunged them into total darkness. They worked on just the same, clearing the deck, moving the wounded into the fo'c'sle, passing out water.

Mr Burgess ordered the Africans brought on deck in groups of ten. As each ten came up he asked them in a clear voice if any of them spoke English. The fourth time he asked, a man stepped forward and answered in a quiet voice, 'I speak it, sir.'

A stunned silence fell across the deck. None of the sailors had ever considered that the Africans they were going to sell like animals might actually speak their own tongue.

'Strike off that man's chains.'

Eli Twiss came painfully out of the shadow where he had been dozing and went below for a hammer and chisel. In the meantime Dónal remembered that Mr Munro had a key for the padlock and he ran to the quarterdeck. The mate struggled to prevent him searching his pockets but Dónal found the keys easily enough. By the time Eli came creaking back on deck the African was free.

'Now, sir,' said Mr Burgess. 'I will explain to you what has happened. You understand?'

The African nodded his head to signify that he did.

'Very well. I have taken command of this ship. I intend to free every one of your people. But before I do that I must have your promise. A promise, you understand?'

'I understand.'

'You must promise not to turn on us. Not to attack us. We are the only ones who can sail the ship back to your country. If you kill us you will die too, understand?'

'I will tell my people and we will promise.'

'I thank you, sir.'

All through the dark hours the Africans were brought

on deck and had their chains unlocked. The clank of falling metal was so loud that Dónal believed it would be heard on the distant ship. Every so often the chains were thrown over the side. Then the Africans began to sing, sitting on the crowded deck, at first in low voices, then louder, until their voices filled the night and seemed to drive back the darkness. At first Mr Burgess tried to get them to stop but after repeated fruitless efforts he gave up. 'I reckon they deserve to sing, if that's what they want, Dónal.'

Now they learned that the African who spoke English had lived in the house of an Arab merchant in Porto-Novo. There he had learned to speak several languages, 'but only French and English of the European tongues. My people have always spoken languages.' He had worked for the merchant, buying and selling ivory and gold, but had never mastered the skill of accounting. He spoke well and when he could not supply a word in English he used a French one so that they could understand him at all times. His name was Karaku and he was, he told them, a warrior of the Edo tribe, which had once governed all of Benin and much more besides. His language was Edo, but he spoke and understood all the other branches of the Kwa language that were spoken in Benin, as well as Arabic. He had been on a visit to the home of his father when the Dahomey slave factor had taken him. This was a thing that not even the King of Dahomey would do because Karaku was a nobleman of his family. His father, two brothers and a sister had died in the barracoons, so he had every reason to hate the slavers.

Mr Burgess explained briefly to him what was happening, how the ship that was coming up astern might be a pirate ship and how the pirates would certainly enslave them all again, white and black. His men would man the guns for as long as they could, but if the pirates boarded them it would be every man for himself. Karaku drew himself up and declared that his people would fight as well as any white man and maybe better.

'But I must have you below decks while the guns are in use. Your people do not understand the cannons.'

'Never.'

'Nay, they must go below. Out of sight.'

After some argument in which Mr Burgess assured him that if he had meant to enslave them again he would never have taken off their chains, Karaku agreed to speak to them.

An hour later the sun was above the eastern horizon and the ship was clearly outlined against it. The Africans had again returned to their slave deck, though free men now, and at least they were not restricted by chains. Their whispered conversation drifted up through the gratings. Mr Munro was locked in his cabin, still bound hand and foot.

Now every man on deck stared into the rising sun. It was a sizeable ship, a frigate at least. The sailors guessed at a thirty-two gunner, capable of sinking them in one or two broadsides. Their eyes strained to make out her colours.

The *Provident* was dead in the water, not a scrap of sail aloft, and the frigate bore down on them rapidly, throwing off a fine bow-wave. Mr Burgess lit the slow match for Dónal, and Gideon Blood crouched in the foretop cradling his musket. The gun crews stood by their guns, bracing them with the tackles against the rolling of the ship.

'Aloft there,' Mr Burgess shouted. 'What colours does she wear, Gideon Blood?'

'Cain't see,' was the reply.

'It's a damn pirate, I know it.'

Dónal thought of their last encounter, where they had won a fine victory. They had had luck on their side then, and a ship in good trim even though the gunnery was bad. She could sail and turn and make her escape eventually. Now they did not have enough men either to fight or to sail. This time there would really be no fight. This fine, trim ship that was between them and the sun would simply stand off at the right range and pick them off one by one. Then they would board and the unarmed Africans would be no match against pistols and cutlasses and boarding pikes. It would be slaughter.

'I see colours!' Gideon Blood was shouting from the maintop.

'What colours?'

'The sun. I cain't see. Black, I think.'

'Right, men. That's it. Stand to your guns.' The gun crews took their places. 'Stand by now.' The guns were raked backwards so as to fire as soon as the ship came in range, but without the ability to turn the ship there was little hope of hitting anything. 'Steady now.'

Dónal saw the ship clearly and there was something familiar about it, though he could not quite say what. The sun was higher now and they could see that she was well kept, not tattered and dirty like the Barbary pirate. A well kept ship.

'On deck there,' Gideon Blood sounded excited. 'A limey!'

The gun crews gasped. Gideon Blood was swinging down the rigging, his musket slung over his shoulder. Mr Burgess was smiling broadly and clapping Dónal on the back.

'It's a limey, Dónal! A limey!'

'In the name of God, Mr Burgess, what are you talking about?'

'A lime juicer! A British ship. That's what we call a British ship on account of they ship lime juice to keep out the scurvy. She's a frigate I'd say. We're saved.'

But the British ship came on and Dónal saw that all her gunports were open and all her guns run out. She was racing towards them in battle trim, hammocks rolled along the bulwarks to reduce the risk of splinters, marines on the crosstrees, muskets at the ready, gun crews standing with reaming irons and sponges, the slow matches smoking in the buckets. With a shock Dónal realised she was about to fire on them.

'Well, lad,' said Burgess, who clearly had seen only a friendly flag flying from the jack, 'we are saved after all.'

They heard the report of a single shot from below decks.

10

FIRE AS SHE BEARS!

Mr Burgess heard the whole story in the end. Being an officer himself he was invited to dine in the officers' wardroom. Lieutenant Trowbridge told the story after a dinner of fish and salt beef and several bottles of wine followed by a fine tawny-coloured bottle of port.

'I declare, Lieutenant Trowbridge, this is a very fine dinner you have given me. I have not eaten the like since I left America!'

Lieutenant Trowbridge inclined his head to acknowledge the compliment. 'Will I tell you how we came up with you? How we came to fire into you? I blush to think of it.'

'Never you mind, Lieutenant. I would have done the same myself in my naval days.'

'It happened thus. We were cruising to Buenos Aires on the River Plate,' he said, 'sailing down the trade winds into the setting sun, all plain sail set, when the lookout cried that there was something on the starboard bow "very like a ship". An irritated demand to be more exact from Mr Seary, who was officer of the watch at the time, only brought the return that the object on the bow was "very like a hulk with her masts struck down and fair blacked".

'There was nothing for it. I had to climb into the rigging myself, spoiling my stockings with the melted tar, there to stare at the "object" through a telescope. It was indeed very like a ship, and almost a frigate at that. But a ship in a very bad way. The winds were light that day, east northeast, as I recall, and the hulk, if that's what it was, heaved itself up and down on the swell like a drunk pig.

'As we drew closer I could see that it was or had been a sloop of war, that it had been partially destroyed by fire and that this fire was very likely the result of an attack. I needn't tell you the dread with which I apprehended the remains of that fire. Fire at sea, and in these latitudes too, where every timber in the ship is as dry as matchwood! I prayed God it was not an English ship.'

He coughed as he said it and bowed slightly to his guests. 'Pardon my way of saying things,' he said. 'I had not thought of an American ship. I'm sure my sentiment applied to all those who are not enemies of His Majesty's government. Indeed I would not wish that calamity on anyone, enemy or friend.

'I slipped down to the deck again and sent word for the captain. Then I called the yeoman of the signals and told him to stand by in case the captain wanted to signal the hulk. I also sent word to the ship's surgeon that his services might be required and to wait on the captain. Finally I ordered a slight alteration of the course that would bring us within a cable's length of the fire-ship.

'By the time Captain Vale had come on deck all the necessary preparations had been made.

'He stared about him, very angry at being disturbed. "Well, Mr Trowbridge? What is this ship I have been told about?" You know his bluff way of talking, Mr Burgess. He is a gruff man but a fair one.

'"A frigate I think, sir, by her lines," I told him. "But lines are all that are left of her. She has been on fire. Top hamper all gone. Stern and forecastle all but burnt away. A woeful fire, I should think."

'"Very well, bring us alongside, or near enough to hail them."

'"I have already altered course, sir."

'"Excellent, Mr Trowbridge. In that case call me again when we are near. Oh, and have the surgeon wait on me. No doubt there will be sick."

'"Surgeon to wait on you, sir, aye."'

The *Badger* drew down on the black ship at a steady pace, according to Mr Trowbridge, but it was an hour or more before they called the captain. By then every man on board knew that this ship was an example of one of their deepest dreads. They could see the charred and blackened timbers, the huge hole where a quantity of powder had blown out through the larboard side, the heavy movement that told them the ship was slowly settling into the sea. There were no bodies, though there was plenty of timber floating on the swell. They knew that with such a fire the crew would have thrown anything that would float into the sea and then jumped in after it to escape the blistering heat and certain death on the decks.

'Close to, we could see why there were no bodies – the deadly hooked fins cruising back and forth, hoping for more. We cursed the sharks.

'"What do you make of her, Trowbridge?" asked the captain.

'"Hard to say, sir. Not much left. Shall I take a boat across?"

'"Carry on, Mr Trowbridge."

'"Very good, sir. There may be some survivors."

'As we pulled towards it,' the lieutenant said, gazing steadily at his glass of port, 'I reflected that had anyone survived they would be leaping up and shouting at us by now.'

Standing up in the boat, Mr Trowbridge explained, he could see that the decks had burned through, and so had most of the bulwarks and rails. On the starboard side the remains of the two masts, charred through below the crosstrees, lay canted into the sea. There were no bodies here either. Quite clearly no one could survive so vicious a blaze, on deck or below. He brought the boat round to the gaping hole on the larboard side, now no more than six inches above the swell. The hull was almost full of water.

'I hallooed into the shadows and heard only the ghostly echo of my own voice. There was no living thing on the hulk.

'"Pull for the *Badger*," I told the oarsmen.

'I did not like the smell, and I felt that there were fevers lurking there. As soon as I had made my report we made sail again.

'"I shall not waste shot in sinking her, Trowbridge,"

said Captain Vale. "I should think she will be long gone to Davey Jones before any other ship happens this way. What do you make of her?"

'"It's a puzzle, sir. A merchant perhaps? No sign of a slave deck. But no sign of cargo either."

'But the captain did not think so. "No, sir. Not a merchant, nor yet a naval vessel. A pirate."

'I may as well tell you that I was shocked by that,' Trowbridge told Mr Burgess, 'and I asked him what he meant by it. I had never seen a pirate, you see.'

Mr Burgess said that he had met one but recently and it was an encounter he did not wish to repeat in his lifetime.

'Indeed. But Captain Vale has been in these waters before and in those around Algezir and such places where they abound.

'He pointed out the likely features to me. "A fast ship, yes? Possibly a frigate, naval at one time. Her lines speak of fast passages. French built. Captured in North Africa or off the coast there. What's she doing here? Lying in wait for slavers. Good pickings." He smiled briefly. You may have noticed that he is not a man much given to smiling. "But," says he, "she met her match." That was you, but we did not know it at the time.

'"You think so?" said I.

'"Indeed she must have. Shot-holes, you saw them. Someone hit the magazine I'd say. Not much powder in there, just enough to attack the occasional merchantman. Enough to blow a hole in her but not enough to blow her up. Set her afire. Well, good luck to them whoever struck her. I can't abide a pirate. I hate them above all else."

'By now darkness had fallen and the wind had almost fallen away with it. I busied myself with crowding on as much sail as the yards would carry - studding sails, sky sails, water sails - so that it seemed that every scrap of air that came our way was trapped in some piece of canvas or other. Then it was time for supper and my watch below. I dined well enough on salt beef and small beer and turned into my berth still puzzling over the hulk.

'The wardroom steward woke me two hours later. It was six bells and the captain wanted me topsides, he told me.

'I cursed the captain and struggled sleepily into my clothes, threw a cloak over my shoulders and came on deck. The captain and Mr Seary stood by the starboard rail staring out over the sea. It was a moonlit night, you may recall. I was annoyed to see that Seary, who had taken over the watch from me, had seen fit to reduce sail until we were barely moving.

'"You called me, sir?" There was an edge to my voice, I'm sure.

'The captain merely gestured towards the bow. By straining my eyes I was able to make out a black shape in the distance.

'"Not another blasted hulk!"

'"No indeed, Mr Trowbridge. Pray use my perspective glass."

'The captain handed me a telescope and through its single powerful eye the moonlight revealed the shadow of a ship, whole and entire it seemed, and not burned at all. Certainly its yards were not squared off, she had no sail up and there was no sign of life aboard. But she was not a hulk.

'"What think you?"

'"A pirate again, sir?" We did not think to find an American vessel in such a way, wallowing so dreadful on the swell, yards awry. More port, Burgess? Indeed it is a capital fine port.

'Anyway the captain inclined to agree with me about the ship being a pirate. "Very likely one of their scurvy damn tricks," he told me. "We will clear for action at eight bells," says he. "You see I have shortened sail. I intend to come up with them at dawn. The moon will go down shortly." And I had thought it was Seary who had taken in the sail out of timidity. It was well that I did not complain of it aloud.'

Lieutenant Trowbridge described how at eight bells in the middle watch they cleared the ship for action. The portholes were opened and the great guns loaded and run out. Battle lanterns were hung on the beams over their heads, but not lit. The slow matches were passed around and then each hand was served a tot of rum.

Just before dawn the captain ordered all plain sail and the crew went about the task silently, each man thinking that this ship they were bearing down on would be theirs in an hour or two. A prize crew would be put aboard and she would be sailed to Africa or South America, there to be sold to the highest bidder. Every man on board would have his fair share of that prize. Pirate ships were especially valued prizes, in the opinion of naval sailors, not only because of the navy's traditional hatred of pirates, but also because they were thought to contain treasure. This notion persisted although none of them had ever heard directly of a rich pirate or of a man-of-war that had been enriched by capturing one.

Dawn came suddenly. A brightening of the eastern sky was the warning, followed almost immediately by the sun itself, which spread its light over the sea and revealed the enemy exactly where it should have been. A small adjustment of course brought her fine on the larboard bow so that as they passed her they would be able to rake her with shot. Now each gun captain tended his gun, making sure that all was ready. The guns were out on both sides because the captain had decided that if the enemy ship did not make sail they would wear ship and run down her other side raking that with a second broadside.

'We were coming down on her very fast now and still the ship showed no sign of making sail. Nor did she fly any flag. Not only were her yards disgracefully crooked, but there were scraps of unfurled sail on them. I determined that something was wrong. It was not well, you see. What ship, even a merchant vessel, would lie about in the trades like that?'

Through his telescope, Trowbridge explained, he could see that there were men standing on deck, staring at them. Just as the captain gave the order to stand to the guns, he realised that this was not a trick, but a genuine ship in distress.

'"Do not fire, Captain."

'"I beg your pardon, sir?"

'I told him I believed the ship was distressed, that I was certain of it, in fact. "Heave to, I beg you."

'I heard the captain's intake of breath even above the sound of the ship preparing for action and the heaving of the canvas. "I beg to differ with you, Trowbridge. She is yet another detestable pirate and this is a detestable scurvy trick. See, her guns are run out. She is cleared for action. She is showing no flag. Stand to your guns, Mr Trowbridge."

'An order cannot be ignored, as you know, Burgess. I am sorry for it, we struck you hard I know, and many of your people suffered for it. I am heartily sorry for it, but an order is an order even on board of a merchant. Or so they say anyway. "Stand to the guns it is, sir," I replied. I turned to the master gunner in the waist of the ship and repeated the order and heard it repeated in turn along the gun deck, that dread I spoke of earlier rising to good effect about my heart.

'No sooner had the ship fallen silent again than the noise of a shot came to us across the water. Captain Vale looked pointedly at me and raised his eyebrows. I knew what he was thinking, and it looked bad I must say. For, do you see, if you were a distressed slaver what business had you letting off shots?

'"That was a shot, I think," he said to me. "You may fire as she bears, Mr Trowbridge."

'"Fire as she bears it is, sir."

'The order was repeated. The gunners bent to the gunports, waiting for the pirate ship to swim into view. We were bent on your destruction and precious little could I say to prevent it.

'The captain began to explain the niceties of naval broadsides to Mr Seary, who had never heard a gun fired in anger yet. He explained how once the ship came in view each gunner would fire. How the cannonballs travelled upwards a little at first, then curved downwards, crashing into the timbers of the ship opposite. "At least that is what we all earnestly hope. If the range is not right, or the elevation of the gun, then the shot will fall long or short as the case may be. Before the gunners can load and fire again the enemy ship may slip past and then it will be necessary to turn and come down the far side. Since the enemy ship is not moving, except a little from the effect of wind on her hull and in her masts and yards and rigging, we shall have no difficulty in firing a second time at her, Mr Seary. No difficulty at all. Altogether," the captain concluded, "a very satisfactory piece of gunnery practice."

'Suddenly the great guns boomed, the air was filled with smoke, the ship shuddered underfoot. It is such a tremendous thing, indeed, a broadside. When the smoke cleared, Mr Seary was invited by the captain to observe the very satisfactory result. Across the way and slipping rapidly astern, your ship was bursting into life. People were spilling onto your decks in vast numbers. The foremast was tottering on its base and likely to go by the board at any moment. We had done considerable damage to your hull and rigging. I confess I was impressed by the accuracy of our fire, albeit you were a sitting bird.

'"Oh capital! Capital!" cries Mr Seary clapping his hands together in delight, the idiot! "Capital shooting, sir. My congratulations!"

'"Indeed," the captain replied, studying the effect through his telescope. "I do believe in keeping the gunnery up to the mark." Which he does, God bless him.'

A RUM LOOKING WHITE MAN

After the battle it was touch and go for two weeks whether Mr Burgess would live or die. The amputation had been terrible. Dónal had stayed as long as he could, speaking quietly to the mate in the yellow light of the lanterns, encouraging him. He had seen him fed a prodigious amount of brandy so that he sang songs and told jokes despite the pain in his arm. Then Dónal had seen him strapped to the table, arms, legs and body. He had seen the surgeon's knives, of every shape and size, his saws no better than and no different from the saws poor old Eli Twiss had used on board the *Provident*. He had seen the surgeon's bloody hands, his blood-spattered apron. But when the knife went into Mr Burgess's shoulder he could no longer stay. He stood outside the sickbay listening to the mate's drunken moans and did not return until the surgeon's mate came out to tell him that his friend's arm was gone. Indeed, the surgeon's mate had the shattered arm in a bucket as he spoke.

Then Dónal sat by Mr Burgess's side throughout the

raging fever that followed the operation, feeding him water, talking to him, listening to his rambling talk of Boston, his wife and children, his seafaring and the hated slave trade.

When at last the mate's fever abated and he was able to understand what was being said to him, Dónal told him what had happened after that single terrible broadside.

Having been aboard a man-of-war preparing to fire, Dónal recognised the signs sooner than anyone else on the *Provident*. He saw the guns, the eager faces at the gunports, the officers passing the orders. He threw himself on the deck shouting for Burgess and the others to do the same just as the enormous crash of the broadside reached their ears. Gideon Blood, slow and careful as he usually was, hit the deck almost as fast as Dónal. Eli Twiss was very fast up in the rigging, moving nimbly along the ropes like a much younger man, but down on the deck his ancient bones creaked like rigging in a gale. A ball caught him at the waist and killed him on the spot, bursting his body in two in the process. Mr Burgess was too slow. A ball took him suddenly by the arm, spun him round and crashed him onto the deck. From where he lay, Dónal could see the shattered remains of his elbow, the blood streaming out of it, and nothing but a lump of meat where the forearm should have been.

It was all over in an instant. Dónal heard the straining of the foremast which was about to fall down, the groaning of the wounded among the guns, the sound of the ship's timbers creaking on the swell.

Then the Africans spilled onto deck, about fifty of

them, not in disorder but with some military purpose in mind. They quickly picked up any weapons that were lying on deck and formed a soldierly rank on the starboard side, weapons at the ready. Karaku was holding Gideon Blood's giant musket in a fashion that indicated he knew what he was doing. The others had reaming irons, cutlasses, knives – warlike, dignified, prepared to fight even against the fearfully uneven odds. As he watched, they began to chant in a powerful resonant voice, swaying and stamping their feet as they did so, and Dónal had time to wonder what he and Gideon Blood would have done had they been faced with fighting off this disciplined unit instead of the slave factor's disorganised brutes.

But Gideon Blood was on his feet, manhandling a cannon to point it at the British ship, and Dónal followed him.

'They done fired at us!'

'It must be a mistake, Gideon.'

The Kentuckian growled and put his shoulder to the gun. 'I'm a-going to shoot their head off if its the last thing I do! Damned limey cowards!'

Dónal looked around desperately. There were wounded men everywhere. Eli Twiss was dead, Burgess dying. He had no doubt the carnage below in the slave deck was enough to drive Karaku to madness, but at least he would see that he had not been tricked since the white men had suffered so cruelly too.

'The captain will know what to do,' he thought. He dashed for the companion, jumped the steps of the ladder and rushed at the captain's door, only to find it firmly sealed shut.

'Captain! Captain! We are under attack! We must stop it!' But before he had shouted the last word he knew what he must do. The signal locker contained all the neatly folded signal flags as well as the big American flag that he had first seen so long ago off the south coast of Ireland. He dragged it from its shelf and rushed on deck. A glance on the lee showed him that the British ship was still holding her course ahead of them. She would turn soon and come down the other side, firing as she came. There would be more death.

In an instant he was in the ratlines of the mainmast, climbing for all he was worth.

The officers of the *Badger* saw him, a boy with more sense than the men aboard, climbing like a monkey with the American flag draped over his shoulder.

'I say, that's plucky,' Trowbridge exclaimed.

'A clever boy, worth more than all his officers,' was Captain Vale's estimate.

Mr Seary was wondering whether, under the circumstances, he would have had the brains to think of a thing like that. His schoolmasters had always said he was a dunce, and he had always been inclined to believe them. He felt lucky and privileged to have found a profession where being a dunce was not considered too much of a handicap.

'Pray God he does not lose his footing in his speed.' Mr Trowbridge and Captain Vale had the same thought.

Dónal stood now on the crosstrees of the mainmast, extending his arms so that the Stars and Stripes blew out on the breeze, a signal for all to see. He stared at the British ship for some recognition of the signal, saw a man run to the mast, and saw the Union Jack fall from its place, dip to halfway and rise again. The British ship had saluted him. She was heaving to. He could see sailors backing the jib, bracing the topsails, straining at the complicated manoeuvre, in which the sails were so arranged that one half of them pushed the ship forward while the other half forced her back so that the ship was brought to a halt.

'On deck,' he shouted down. 'She's heaving to. They're lowering a boat.'

It took all his skill to persuade Karaku that the approaching boat was not a boarding party come to fight hand to hand. He seemed genuinely disappointed that he and his warriors would not have a chance to exact revenge for the loss of life below decks, but his discipline was never in doubt. His warriors stacked their weapons against the mainmast and squatted in the shade on his word.

By the time the British officer, who introduced himself as Lieutenant Trowbridge, came on board, they were lifting the wounded from below and laying them out in whatever shade they could find. The shot had ripped through the planking, scattering splinters and chain as it went, and the wounds were horrific.

The first words that Lieutenant Trowbridge uttered were: 'Where is the captain?'

Then Dónal recollected the sound of the shot he had heard just before the broadside and his face paled with shock.

'Are you all right, boy?'

'Come with me, sir. I fear there has been mischief.'

As they made their way to the cabin, Dónal explained about the shot, and Lieutenant Trowbridge remarked that on board the *Badger* they had taken it as a signal to attack.

It took the shoulders of two strong marines to push the door open. The captain had wedged his sea-chest against it and jammed it in place with a boathook. They would not have been able to force it but that the boathook snapped under the marines' strength. Inside, the captain lay dead on his bed, a pistol on the floor beside him. There was a small round hole in his nightshirt, blackened by powder and red with blood. The ship's log lay open on the chart table with a scribbled note half-folded on it.

It is no good. The opium devil has a hold of me.
Trachoma has blinded me and I will never set foot on a
deck again. I am no use to family or country. Goodbye,
Davey. If you live, say I died in the battle. You are the
best seaman I have sailed with. I hope you make your
master's ticket. You would if my name could get it for
you, for I do not hold against you that you took my
command from me. You had good reason.

Nathaniel Pearson

The surgeon attended to each of the wounded in turn and it was late evening before he could tell Dónal that Mr Burgess's shattered arm would have to be taken off. The first mate was conscious by then, and able to tell the tale of the voyage. Lieutenant Trowbridge listened to the story of the opium-eating captain, the murderous second mate, the seizing of the ship, the mutiny, the fight with the slaver. Every now and then Dónal or Gideon Blood threw in their part. But Mr Burgess weakened rapidly and before the tale could end he had fallen asleep, his face pale and yellowed as the sailcloth they had wrapped him in.

'As you see, sir, he is an honest man,' Dónal said.

'Indeed, I believe him,' Mr Trowbridge replied. 'Pray, continue the tale if you can.'

Dónal described how he and Mr Burgess, Gideon Blood and Eli Twiss, had determined to sail the ship back to Africa to deliver their captives into freedom. He explained how Karaku had come forward and had led the Africans in preparing for battle.

'I must fulfil our promise to them, Mr Trowbridge. I cannot allow them to be brought into slavery.'

Mr Trowbridge thought for a while.

'She is not a lawful prize because we are not at war with America. In that case, you know, we have broken the law in firing on her at all. Captain Vale is in a bit of a stew over that. If the Americans decide to make trouble he will be severely reprimanded, perhaps he may even lose his command. It is possible that we may be able to do something yet.'

Lieutenant Trowbridge did everything by the book. He had Mr Munro brought on deck and unbound. Munro took heart on seeing the grey-faced shell of a man that had been Mr Burgess, wrapped in sailcloth that was slowly reddening with blood. He immediately began to complain that the ship had been illegally seized by the first mate, that he had turned the swivel gun on the crew and that Captain Pearson would witness all of what he said.

'Would it surprise you to hear that I do not believe a word you say?' Lieutenant Trowbridge watched him carefully as he spoke.

'Before God, sir, I speak not a word of a lie. Captain Pearson will witness that I was loyal and led the loyal men in an unlucky fight.'

'Captain Pearson is dead by his own hand I'm afraid,' Lieutenant Trowbridge told him, 'and consequently cannot witness anything. However, in his suicide note he made it clear that the first mate, Burgess, whom you accuse, was in fact correct in his actions. On the contrary, it seems that you were the mutineer, by the account of Mr Burgess, seaman Blood and the ship's boy, Long. How say you?'

Munro looked from one face to the next, hatred filling his eyes as he turned from the British officer to Dónal to Gideon Blood.

'You have ruined me.'

Gideon Blood's face split into a huge grin. 'Reckon you done ruined yourself, Munro!'

'I'm afraid Blood is right,' Trowbridge added. 'You have ruined yourself.'

Captain Vale agreed to Trowbridge's plan.

The plan was to put a skeleton crew aboard the *Provident*, just enough men to sail her. Then both ships were to work back through the trade winds to the coast of Africa. They would take the ship to Freetown and sell it there, and the remaining crew would be paid off, the captain's share to be paid to his widow in Boston.

'That,' said Davey Burgess, 'is the best of it. We'll turn the slaves loose in Freetown. Afterwards Cap'n Vale has mighty kindly offered to give me passage to the River Plate. And you, if you'll ship with me.'

'But what about the Africans, Davey? Will they not be enslaved again in Freetown?' Burgess had long ago forbidden Dónal to call him anything but Davey: 'No more misters between us, Dónal. We're shipmates now and we're bound by ties of friendship.'

'It's like this, Dónal,' he was now explaining. 'Way back, twenty years ago I reckon, the limeys – that's British to you – the limeys set up this here Freetown and turned all the slaves they could find loose in it. They got their own life there now. They even got their own language. Krio I believe they call it. Half English, half African. Every slave that runs away makes for Freetown.'

'But why not put them ashore in their own country?'

'Where is their country? Karaku is a fine man but I declare he ain't got so much as penny's worth of navigation. Don't think that the place we picked them up from is their home. That place belongs to our friend the slave factor.'

Dónal was troubled. 'But to leave them so far from their own country and in a town too, when not one of them but Karaku has ever seen a town.'

'It ain't the best thing, but what's done can't be undone. We cain't take them back. So what else can we do? If we put these Africans ashore, God knows where, wherever Cap'n Vale's navigation fetches up, they will be maybe two or three hundred miles from home. Who knows but they might be taken up again by some other slaver. Now, it ain't as easy as it seems. It has to be Freetown, Dónal. And there's Munro. Bad as he is, I don't want to see him at the tail-end of a rope.'

Dónal had no taste for hanging either.

'All round, Dónal, there ain't an easy answer.'

Burgess shifted his position to ease his arm a little. 'What I want to know is what happened to that damned uncle of yourn?'

Dónal shrugged. He supposed that Michael Long had fallen into the hands of the Africans, who would have had every reason to kill him and slip him quietly over the side. He had searched the ship for him and his body had not been found, and there was no other explanation.

Karaku joined them.

'Well, Karaku? Have you decided?' Dónal always drew a smile from Karaku.

'I think I will ask the cap'n,' Karaku replied. He liked the casual way that Mr Burgess spoke and he had picked up a few of his American ways of speaking. He never said 'captain' now, but always 'cap'n'. He even said 'ain't' instead of 'isn't'.

Burgess slapped him on the back and shook his hand. 'You'll make a fine sailor, Karaku. A warlike sailor. Why don't you hang on a bit and join the Continental Navy as we call it back home – we have some mighty fine frigates – the *Constitution* and such like. More'n six of them.'

Karaku smiled broadly. 'I think the King of England has countless ships. I will go with this one and I will learn the ways of the sea.'

Dónal warned him that life on board a man-of-war was hard.

'Hardness is no stranger to me or my people. It is just a different kind of life.'

'What about you, Dónal?' Burgess looked closely at him.

'I cannot think I will ever reach America. But I have decided to throw in my lot with you, Davey. I will go to the River Plate with you.' Burgess was delighted. 'But Gideon Blood has made up his mind to volunteer along with Karaku. He hopes to become a marine, and with his sharpshooting he won't have much trouble.'

Karaku was entered in the list as 'volunteer' by Captain Vale, an entry that gave him higher pay than a 'pressed man' as he gleefully told anyone who asked. Gideon Blood appeared resplendent in a marine's red uniform which had a small black hole in the chest ('Chap who had this on don't need it no more,' he had been told).

The two ships pushed ahead, beating into the wind that had pushed them cheerfully westwards not long before. They settled down to the routine of shipboard life and, under the care of the *Badger*'s surgeon, Mr Burgess's health improved steadily. By the time the lookout raised the cry of 'Land ho!' the mate was stumping about the deck, observing the seamanship of his hosts and dining in the wardroom with Trowbridge, Seary and the purser.

They dropped anchor off a low marshy inlet. This, Lieutenant Trowbridge told them, was Sierre Leon, and just beyond the swamp was the busy port of Freetown. He would send Mr Seary and a party of marines to speak to the authorities and he could promise that Karaku's people would be well looked after. The captain had decided to land them here rather than bringing them into the port itself because he wanted them to land in open country, not among shipping and sailor's haunts and warehouses. Then they could gradually grow accustomed to the sights and sounds of a town.

That night the Africans had their last meal on board the *Provident*. There was singing and dancing on deck, and Dónal, Mr Burgess, Gideon Blood and the officers were invited back from the *Badger* to their old ship, Karaku issuing the invitation.

The sailors too had their feast – fresh fruit brought aboard on the ship's boats, clean water from a stream, fresh meat even. It was a feast day for everyone and Captain Vale said that such days were good for a crew and made them all the more content in the hard times.

Next morning the ship's boats were lowered away and the work of bringing the Africans ashore began. The boats came and went all day as the crowd on the beach grew and that on deck dwindled. The transfer was supervised by Mr Seary and Mr Trowbridge, so it was Mr Seary who brought them the news that 'a rum looking white man' had been found. 'Stowed himself in a locker where the spare sailcloth was kept.' The 'rum looking white man' turned out to be Dónal's uncle. Brought over to the *Badger* in a boat, he wheedled and begged and apologised and wept until he made himself so obnoxious that he was sent back again. He had hidden during the mutiny, when he judged that the fight was going against Munro, and he had fed himself on scraps stolen from the galley ever since.

'We will provision in Freetown, Mr Seary. Let him be turned loose when we get there,' the captain ordered. 'I will not have such a vile man on my deck again.'

His uncle had never been a likeable man. In earlier days he had bullied and flogged Dónal till he feared for his life. Then he had thrown in his lot with the mutineers, wrongly thinking that he was on the winning side. So Dónal was not sorry to part with him. Worse things might have befallen him than to be put ashore near a prosperous town – he might have been hanged for mutiny. Nevertheless the parting was not easy. Michael Long wept again and said he was ashamed that he had let Dónal down, but Dónal was not to be taken in this time. He shook hands with him coldly and expressed the hope that wherever he next found employment he would not betray his friends so foolishly.

'Ah, Dónal, Dónal. Have you no pity for a poor old man? Your own father's brother, that raised you like his own true son in your time of need?'

Dónal remembered the beatings this same uncle used to give him and he looked away in disgust. 'I wish you well,' he said coldly. 'And that's more than you deserve. I am a sailor now and I must find my own way in the world. Goodbye.'

He held out his hand but his uncle merely looked at it. At first Dónal thought he was going to cry, but instead he burst into a string of curses, finishing with, 'You were always an ungrateful brat! May you have bad luck for the rest of your days!'

They separated on those terms, Dónal to the *Badger*, his uncle to find his way to Freetown. They would not meet again for a long time.

And so finally Dónal Long and Davey Burgess were bound for Buenos Aires and the River Plate. At times it seemed to Dónal that the burden of his past was already too much for a boy to bear – the struggles of his boyhood days, the loss of his parents and friends, the terrible shame of the slaving voyage. Now more than ever he felt the need of the cleaning sweep of the ocean, something that might help to clear from his mind the vision of hell that had been given to him – the burning pirate ship, the murderous second mate, the cruelty he had witnessed in the name of economy, the blind and opium-addicted captain, the battles and killings and the death of friends.

'There can hardly be anything worse in store for me,' he told himself. 'I have lived through the worst that can befall a man. After this things can only get better.'